NEW YORK TIMES and USA TODAY Bestselling Author

Lora Leigh

12/09

Aiden's Charity

ELLORA'S CAVE
ROMANTICA PUBLISHING

What the critics are saying...

৪০

"The Breeds are back and they are just as Alpha as ever. [...] This is most definitely a Keeper. Ms. Leigh should be an auto buy for any reader interested in a well-written spellbinding read. Bravo Ms. Leigh!" ~ *Just Erotic Romance Reviews*

"AIDEN'S CHARITY is the latest installment in the Breed series. [...] I can hardly wait for the next. [...] The development of their romance kept me turning the pages to get to the next heated fight." ~ *Sensual Romance Reviews*

An Ellora's Cave Romantica Publication

www.ellorascave.com

Aiden's Charity

ISBN 9781419954467
ALL RIGHTS RESERVED.
Aiden's Charity Copyright © 2003 Lora Leigh
Cover art by Syneca.

This book printed in the U.S.A. by Jasmine-Jade Enterprises,
LLC

Electronic book Publication 2003
Trade paperback Publication June 2007

About the Author

ℵ

Lora Leigh is a wife and mother living in Kentucky. She dreams in bright, vivid images of the characters intent on taking over her writing life, and fights a constant battle to put them on the hard drive of her computer before they can disappear as fast as they appeared.

Lora's family, and her writing life co-exist, if not in harmony, in relative peace with each other. An understanding husband is the key to late nights with difficult scenes, and stubborn characters. His insights into human nature, and the workings of the male psyche provide her hours of laughter, and innumerable romantic ideas that she works tirelessly to put into effect.

Lora welcomes comments from readers. You can find her website and email address on her author bio page at www.ellorascave.com.

Tell Us What You Think

We appreciate hearing reader opinions about our books. You can email us at Comments@EllorasCave.com.

AIDEN'S CHARITY

ෙ

Dedication

ॐ

For Tony, because you made me who I am.

*You gave me freedom, yet held me with
velvet chains of the heart.*

*You gave me love and taught me
that nothing, not even emotion, is perfect.*

*You gave me conflict and made
me search for solutions.*

*You made me strong.
You gave me the strength to
search within myself to find my own peace.*

*You made me listen to the voices, and in
listening, made me see my inner person.*

*You gave me the time, and the strength
to reach out for my dream.
And in doing so, you gave me the
gift of acceptance.*

Prologue
Breed Labs
Mexico

ഔ

He had managed to fool them for years. He had controlled his sexuality, his desires, his automatic attraction to the beauty of the female form. He had withstood their drugs that were designed to make his cock hard and make the sexual training go smoother for the females and the scientists. He had achieved no erections to satisfy any of them. He had no desire, either physically or mentally, sober or drugged, until he saw her. Until the day they introduced the new Lab Tech.

She was young. As small and delicate as anything he had ever seen. Her long, dark blonde hair was like a fall of silk down her back, her large brown eyes watching the cells warily, as though afraid ravening beasts would attempt to escape at any moment.

Her reaction had amused him at first. As the year went by it grated on his conscience, on his emotions. And he couldn't stop watching her, couldn't stop wishing. But he knew the path of revealing such emotions. And as time went by, his rage grew. His anger toward the scientists, the guards, the lives they were forced to live, festered inside him.

The animal in him howled out in fury. The need to survive, to fight for another day, was like a demon ripping at his defiance of the drugs and the tests. But something more primal, some knowledge so basic and ingrained he could not fathom its source, warned him of the dangers to come. Warned him of the threat one woman represented.

He watched her secretly as the new drug coursed through his system that day. Their new aphrodisiac. It was a powerful one this time, taking all his concentration to fight to keep his erection down. Inside he howled in fury. The confinement was bad enough, the constant training to kill; the drugs and experiments were weighing on them all, but even worse was the fury beginning to fill him. It was even harder to control than the drugs, or his desire for this one woman.

That anger was becoming such a part of his soul that there were times Aiden feared it himself. That anger could become a threat to the entire Pack. If he dared to strike out at a guard or one of the inhuman scientists, then the punishment would fall not just on his head, but on the entire Pack. And that thought he found more frightening than any other.

As the anger had grown inside him, he noticed that Charity watched him more often. After more than a year in the Labs she had grown more comfortable with the Breeds. She talked to his sister, Faith. Laughing over whatever girlish things she could fill Faith's head with. As though his sister needed to find hope in this dismal life they led. Unless they found a way to escape, they would all eventually die. If not on one of the perverse missions they were sent on, then by the simple means of their guards' bullets. It had happened before, he was certain it would happen again.

"Aiden?" She approached his cell warily now, her dark eyes worried, her expression somber. "Dr. Bainesmith wants you to service the woman soon."

Compassion and something more glittered in her eyes. He growled, a low sound of warning that had her flinching as she bit her lip nervously. He couldn't contain his rage this time. He wanted this woman, wanted her above all things, and he could not betray that basic, inherent desire to touch none but her. And he feared for her if he did touch her. How would he maintain his control? Death was preferable to this endless maze of wakening emotion and hopeless weakness.

"Aiden, she will have you killed," she whispered imperatively. "Faith will be alone then."

12

The soft sound of her voice was destructive. Like summer's heat it stroked over his senses. His cock rippled with the need to lengthen. He bared his teeth, raising his head enough that she could see the savagery of his expression past the long fall of his hair.

But she wasn't watching his face. Her gaze was trained on his cock. His fickle flesh twitched, but remained limber. He bared his teeth in a silent snarl of warning. Her gaze rose to him slowly, and he saw the knowledge in her eyes. She knew it was he controlling his erection, not the impotence the others believed afflicted him. But there was none of the fear she should have felt.

"Aiden, you can't die," she whispered, glancing over her shoulder to be certain they were alone. "Please, don't continue to defy them this way."

"You may play lap dog all you wish," he bit out coldly. "I will not breed for these bastards."

Something flashed in her eyes then. Her lips thinned, as though there were something she needed to say, something to reassure him. She held it back with a quick shake of her head.

"This is not a good day to die," she hissed quietly. "Save it for something important."

The flash of stubbornness in her gaze, in her expression, intrigued him. He had never seen the silent steel that flashed there before. As though some inner core of strength sustained her. He envied her that stubbornness.

"One less Breed for them to torture," he sneered back at her, hating her concern, her compassion. Hating his need for her and what he must now do to protect not just his Pack, but her as well. "Why do you come to me this way, girl? I could rip you apart with my bare hands. Come, enter my lair, and I'll prove this to you."

Her eyes darkened, first with fear and then with a strange glimmer of defiance. And his cock twitched again. He wanted her. Needed her as he needed nothing else in his life, and there

13

laid his destruction. To take her would be to give them what he knew they wanted. If he released his control to take another, then he knew he would never find it again. He would know no peace, no ease until he had Charity beneath him, his cock buried so deep inside her he would share her soul. And in doing so he would destroy them both. It was better to choose his own death rather than the destruction of his soul.

"I won't let you die," she bit out. "You have no idea what you're doing here, Aiden."

"Fucking their little brood mare won't keep me alive. I was born to die, Charity. We all were. Some just sooner than others." He wished she would leave him. Turn and walk away, and allow him to face his fate with the strength his pride demanded.

Frustration flashed in her eyes.

"Charity, is he ready?" Bainesmith drew their gazes to the other side of the lab where a gurney was being wheeled in.

Aiden's body tightened as the scent of arousal, strong and drug-induced, reached his nostrils. He grimaced at the scent. It overpowered the faint, fresh scent of Charity's earthy response to him, sickening him with its smell.

The woman was strapped to the bed, her legs raised and spread, held into the metal stirrups that had been unfolded. It was a disgusting display, sickening his soul.

The soldiers that accompanied the perverse doctor moved to his cell door as Charity backed away. Aiden didn't give them the satisfaction of fighting them. He rose to his feet and waited patiently. Every muscle in his body demanded action, demanded that he fight. He controlled it as easily as he did his arousal.

He watched broodingly as Bainesmith, her under-scientists, guards and technicians approached his cell slowly. All eyes focused on his thighs and the limp cock that hung there.

"The bastard still hasn't achieved an erection." Bainesmith was coldly furious as she turned to the scientist that accompanied her. "You assured me it would work this time."

The aging doctor shook his head, perplexed. Dr. Agullera was as perverted and depraved as any human Aiden had heard tell of. The man deserved a painful, bloody death. Right after Bainesmith's, of course. "Perhaps impotence is his problem, and not merely defiance, Dr. Bainesmith. I warned you this could be the case." His lofty superior tone set Aiden's teeth on edge.

The cell door opened slowly as the guards awaited him, weapons held ready as they watched him warily. He contained his triumphant smile. He would die, but he would die knowing they feared him.

Aiden stepped from the cell, aware of the fate awaiting him. Bainesmith had made the promise to him when the drug was injected. The experiments into breeding were imperative for some reason. If he couldn't fuck, then he wouldn't live. He watched the doctor's eyes narrow, and cursed her with an inborn fury he prayed would live after his death.

"You were a perfect specimen," Bainesmith sighed in regret. "It's too bad, Aiden. I won't enjoy killing you, I would have much preferred fucking you."

"Aiden, don't let them do this." Wolfe's voice echoed from the adjoining cell as he heard Faith cry out in fear. "Dammit, I order you not to allow this."

He didn't glance at either of them. Today, despite Charity's belief, was as good a day as any to die.

"Take him to the other room," Bainesmith sighed. "I'll deal with him there."

He heard the resignation in her voice. He didn't fight the guards; he allowed them to push him forward and walked voluntarily to the room of death. They all knew what the room was for. You entered there, you didn't come out.

"No!" Charity turned to the doctor. "You can't kill him, Delia."

Her familiarity with the doctor surprised him. She spoke to her with the ease of a long association. A tone to her voice that demanded, expected to be heard without censure.

Silence filled the Lab as all eyes turned to her. Aiden watched her broodingly, daring her to go further.

"Charity, the animal is of no use to us," Bainesmith bit out, her expression creasing into a frown. "Even the drugs don't work on him. He is not a dependable specimen."

Fear flashed in Charity's eyes. She was pale now, her gaze going between him and Bainesmith.

"But he is." She sounded frantic now. "The stimulation is wrong. He's disgusted by those women...he can't help that. He's not being properly stimulated."

Aiden's stomach dropped as fear flashed hard and heavy in the pit of his stomach.

"I would love to fuck her, Charity," he snarled at her, vowing vengeance if she hindered his final escape. "The equipment just doesn't work."

"He's lying." She turned back to him, and he gritted his teeth at what he saw in her eyes.

At that moment he began to pray. Pray that she had not realized his desire for her, his knowledge that he was but a step away from mating her and giving the bastards what they wanted. A child, a creature they believed would mold more easily than the original Breeds did. It was a knowledge he couldn't hide from himself, but he was determined to hide it from the bastards who had created him.

If he revealed his ability to fuck, then it would only be a matter of time before they attempted to match him with a woman he could not deny. Just as they were attempting to match Wolfe, based on his uncontrolled response to Bainesmith's young daughter. The same with his sister, Faith, and his Packmate, Jacob. Tomorrow Faith was scheduled to be drugged and taken to the other man. The thought of that, as well, was unbearable.

There was no privacy in the Labs. The sexual experiments were carried out before the eyes of all those held within the cells. He would be forced to listen to Faith's cries. Here the mating sounds and know it was destroying her. Just as Faith had been forced to listen to her Pack Leader and Jacob as they had taken the women brought to them. He couldn't imagine her or Charity seeing such a loss of control from him. The blow to his pride, to his soul, would be more than he could bear.

"She's too soft for this job, Bainesmith." He smiled with a tight promise of retribution to the girl. "You should have gotten someone a bit harder. I bet she throws up when she sees blood."

He silently cursed as Bainesmith watched the girl with calculated interest.

"Can you produce a response, Charity?" she asked her coldly.

God no. A shiver of dread worked over his spine. He looked at Charity, knowing in that moment she would destroy him.

"I can." Her voice was faint, fear trembling through the sound of it.

Bainesmith's eyes narrowed. "Chain him to the crossbars. We'll see what she can do."

He fought them then. A roar of fury broke past his lips as the guards began to force him to the metal X built on the other side of the room. He would be restrained, unable to move, unable to fight. If she touched him, if he smelled her arousal, it would all be over with.

The weakness the aphrodisiac produced left him little strength to fight. Muscles were lethargic, lacking power; only his cock would have true strength. If she touched his cock, it would damned well explode in seconds.

Within minutes he was strapped to the crossbar. Arms and legs were buckled down, his waist held tight to the center of the X, helpless. He howled in fury, the sound primal, enraged. There would be payment for this, he swore as he fought the straps. And it would begin with Charity.

"There he is, Charity." Bainesmith waved a hand at his nude, bound body. "Get him hard and he can live another day."

Charity approached him warily as he watched her with raw, unbridled fury. He snarled, the animalistic sound vibrating in his chest and throat as he bared the wicked canines at the side of mouth.

"Don't attempt it," he growled at her, ignoring her frightened expression, the wary set of her body. "Touch me, Charity, and I promise you will pay."

She stared up at him, her brown eyes somber, moist with emotion. That look speared into his soul and tightened his chest with emotions too unfamiliar to delve into.

"I won't let you die." Her hand touched his hard abdomen. "I can't, Aiden."

Her touch had his muscles clenching in pleasure. He growled at her again, his teeth snapping together in warning as her hand trailed lower.

"I'll kill you myself." She was going to go down on him. He saw the clear intent in her eyes and knew he was doomed.

If her soft mouth touched his cock he would not have the strength to fight her. Already his weakened flesh was stirring, overpowering his control, desperate to tempt her into touching it.

"But at least you'll live one more day," she whispered sadly.

Her lips touched his abdomen. He felt the fire lick over his body, the desire that simmered in his blood flaming at the moist touch. His cock tingled, pleading to be free of his control. He gritted his teeth, fighting the lust surging through his loins.

"Just one day," she whispered again against his skin. "That's all you need, Aiden, just one more day."

She went to her knees, the wet heat of her mouth covering his cock as he roared out his fury. Her hand cupped his scrotum, messaging it as her tongue stroked over his flexing cock. He couldn't fight it. Oh God, her mouth was so good. Hot and tight. Her tongue was timid but felt like a whip of fire on his flesh.

He felt his erection blooming. His body tightened as he fought it, but he couldn't fight the drug, and her sweet mouth. As though the moist depths were made for him alone, his cock hardened, lengthened, until she was forced to wrap her hands around the base, covering more than half of the shaft to keep him from strangling her as his hips suddenly bucked, burying the heated length into her mouth.

His mind rioted, his body betraying him as deeply as Charity was. He felt his erection surging as the pleasure began to lick over his body. It was extreme, too intense to resist, too heated to fight any longer. He forgot the depraved scientists watching the act, forgot the soldiers and their perverse amusement. Without conscious control he began to fuck her suckling mouth. The restraints did little to hinder the movement of his hips, did nothing to stop his desperate thrusts into the heated warmth between her lips.

He wanted to touch her. He wanted to stroke and caress her. Years of pent up arousal, of hard won control shattered in that instance. He felt his cock convulse, her mouth tighten. His groan was a cry of tortured pleasure as he felt his seed erupt from the tip.

He blasted into her mouth, his head thrown back, his strangled cry echoing around him as she suckled his seed from him. And still his cock tightened further, a swelling hidden by her hands that increased the ecstasy tearing through his body.

Her hands tightened around the sudden, almost fist sized knot that bloomed within the shaft. She stroked it, her tongue laving the pulsing head of his erection, drawing each violent burst of his semen into the heated depths of her mouth until he felt as though he would go insane from the need to fuck her tight cunt.

It was over too soon, yet Aiden knew it had lasted too long. Her hands eased the hard knot but now nothing could ease the drug-induced arousal that filled his body. His cock was still engorged, so hard it hurt, and the need to fuck overcame any other need his mind held.

He shuddered as she drew back then. Her lips moist, her gaze silently pleading for forgiveness as the cool air of the Lab replaced the wet heat of her mouth.

Aiden hung limply in the straps, his head lowered as he stared at her kneeling before him. Hatred welled within him, fury igniting every nerve ending in his body as he watched her lick the last remaining evidence of his seed from her mouth.

The betrayal was nearly more than he could bear. It pumped hard and fast through his body, searing nerve endings, tightening muscles. Yet, once stimulated, his cock now refused to return to its limber state, though the desperate swelling beneath her hand subsided. She had betrayed him. The reasons why did not matter.

"You will pay," he growled. "Somehow, some way, you will pay."

Her sad little smile was only reinforced by the tears in her eyes. "I already have, Aiden, in ways you will never know."

And he promised himself, one day, she would pay by his hand.

Chapter One
Six years later
Breed Labs, South America

ဆ

Escape. It was a litany within her head. The Labs were exploding around her, the mechanical countdown to the final explosion echoing around her with hollow gloom. The backup generators had finally failed; releasing the lock to the cell she had spent the past months confined in.

Charity paid little attention to her nakedness or the burning pain in the soles of her feet as she rushed across the metal floors. The mountain would collapse when the countdown finished, that she knew. She was on the wrong end of the underground compound to even pray for help. She had been kept isolated after she aided the Winged Breeds in their escape attempt. Placed as far away from them as possible in the hopes that should the others be rescued by their brothers, then she, at least, would remain.

Chemicals exploded around her, broken electrical lines danced in a mad marionette as she rushed through the cavernous rooms. The adrenaline pumping through her system would only move the latest batch of drugs through her body that much quicker. She knew time was running out for her. When the full force of the artificial hormone hit her, she would be too weak, too helpless to protect or save herself.

The air around her heated as the flames became more intense. She could feel her feet burning, blistering from the scalding metal beneath them, and pushed herself to run faster, harder. If she could just reach the escape tunnel in time, then she knew safety would only be moments away.

The dim lighting from the battery-powered lamps guided her, the eerie red glow shedding at least partial illumination on the long corridors that led through the Breeding Labs. Yet the faster she ran, the closer the flames and the heat seemed to get.

She fought for breath, feeling the weakness invading her body, knowing that time was something she didn't have and sure as hell couldn't steal this time. A ragged scream born of fury escaped her throat. Surely her sacrifices wouldn't end in her own death, as she had always feared. She was so close, so close to freedom that she could taste it. Feel it.

She gasped, hope blooming within her as she staggered through the marked exit. The floor was so hot she could feel the knifing pain searing through her ankles as it baked her flesh, but she could feel the cooling breeze on her face.

"Damn you, Aiden," she cried out the curse. She always cursed him when the fear overwhelmed her. It gave her strength, gave her purpose.

He had left her in those damned Labs six years before. Left her aching, needing as he escaped, hoping he would return for her. For years she had nursed that hope inside her.

She had deceived the Council at every turn. Passed information, passed messages, fought for the tortured souls the bastards created, and prayed each day that some miracle would occur to halt the genetic experiments. But they never had. And each day she had prayed he would come for her. Until the prayers slowly stopped, the hope strangled away, and she gave up. She gave up, but her body remembered.

The remembrance he had left inside her had been her downfall. Her punishment. He had sworn she would pay, and she had paid in exacting measures over the years. In the last months, the payment had increased until she feared for her very sanity.

Tears streamed down her face, blurring her vision as she struggled through the last tunnel. The countdown was drawing closer to the final number, the final escape. It would be far easier, she thought distantly, to wait it out, to become another casualty to the desperate battle between science and its creations. But some part of her, some last shred of her survival instinct refused to let her surrender. She had to escape. She had to live. Though for what, she was no longer certain.

Finally, blessedly, the deserted opening to the mountain loomed ahead. The drugs were pumping harder through her body now, weakening her legs, sending pain radiating through her abdomen. She clutched her stomach, fighting to ignore the torturous reaction of her body to the chemicals as she burst through the opening and into the clear night air beyond.

Explosions blasted around her as she screamed out in shock, her hands covering her head as debris rained upon her. A blast of heated air threw her to the ground, but she couldn't stop. She half crawled, half ran to the protection she knew only the jungle could provide. And she kept running.

The shelter of the trees cut even the fragile rays of the moon to the dimmest light, making it nearly impossible to see now. Despite the flames behind her, the inferno bursting through the night sky, here darkness reigned. Cool, soothing, the night air whispered around her, safe and sheltering as she pushed herself through the jungle, forcing her body to put as much distance as possible between her and the exploding Labs.

The soft dirt beneath her feet was like daggers through her flesh as she kept moving. Always moving. Escape. Safety. She had fought for years to escape and had been too terrified of what would happen to those she fought to save. She would die, she swore, before she allowed them to take her back this time. She was doomed now. They knew her secrets, knew the changes slowly occurring in her body. She was of little use to herself, and of no use to the Breeds she had tried to save for so long.

She stumbled into the jungle, her vision faint now as the drugs filled her body. Pain was a brutal reminder that at least she still lived, though why she fought to do so had become the question of the year. She should have given up months ago, she thought sadly. The brutal testing should have killed her, not to mention the stress of blood loss, and the forced transfusions of blood her body no longer wanted to accept.

She fell to her knees. The pain from the abrupt landing merely blended in with the rest of the agony flaring through. She gasped for breath, whimpering as she struggled to keep moving, crying out as she fought the overriding paranoia that the drugs induced. The sounds of the jungle were too loud; the screech of a bird, the shuffle of the wildlife in the brush.

Animals could smell blood. It brought out the scavengers and predators of the night looking for a handy meal. A sobbing laugh escaped her. She would be little more than a diseased snack to any creature unlucky enough to take a bite of her. But she also knew her scent, the smell of her tainted blood, would hold them back. Animals were often much smarter than their human enemies.

She couldn't force herself back to her feet. The weakness of her body was too draining, and it took more strength than she now possessed, so she crawled instead. It eased the pain in her feet, though the fire raging in her womb only grew worse. The incision made in her abdomen that morning was bleeding again. They could never truly halt the bleeding once the drugs were injected inside her.

She couldn't stop the pain, or the need. And in that need she whispered Aiden's name. When the drugs inside her reached their peak, she knew she screamed it out. Screamed and begged for ease, though none ever came. And the bastards who built on whatever Aiden had done to her so many years ago would only strap her to the metal bed, attach the probes to her body and make their little notes.

She hoped they died. She hoped every one of them were in that fucking mountain when it collapsed. Buried in the waste of their own evil. A bark of hysterical laughter escaped her at that thought.

"Sons of bitches," she gasped, fighting to pull herself through the dense undergrowth of the jungle. "I hope they're screaming in pain."

She stopped, her body tightening as she gritted her teeth against the weakness that dropped her further to the ground. She could feel her juices dripping from her body, thick and hot from her greedy cunt. The arousal was more than she could bear now. Her body was hungry, starved for fulfillment, demanding a release that just didn't exist.

"Aiden..." she cried out his name, desperation born of fury, pain and fear echoing in the air around her. It hurt, this need. The pounding fury of sexual hunger was unlike anything she could have imagined.

Damn, it was worse than before. She tightened her thighs, fighting the pain of the arousal. It throbbed through every cell of her body, tightening her muscles to a screaming peak as her womb clenched in need. She could feel the blood running along her abdomen, the rippling pulse in her womb. Just her luck, she thought, she was going to bleed to death before she could ever effectively escape.

Stupid scientists. She had been under their noses for years as they fought to find or to capture a Breed mate. They had kept the semen collected over the years, preserved for use, constantly watching for a candidate for their evil. They had no idea she existed. No idea she had become bound to Aiden the day she had so foolishly swallowed his semen. But, boy, had they tried to make up for lost time after they found out.

She had messed up, allowed them to catch her aiding the Winged Breeds. They had needed a woman at the time to place with the leader, Keegan, and for a while, debated her use. Until they checked her blood, and found what she had found years before. A hormone known only to the Wolf Breeds and a high level of the aphrodisiac reported to run only through the blood of mated females. From that moment on her life had become hell.

"Bastards." Her teeth gritted as her womb convulsed again.

She clamped her hand to the incision in her stomach, praying the bleeding wouldn't become severe again. Sometimes it did. Sometimes, she was certain she would die.

The sounds of gunfire, explosions and the screams of war could still be easily heard. Charity breathed out wearily, knowing she had to move, she had to drag herself farther away from the fighting, the possibility of capture. She wanted to lay down and rest, to forget the horrors of the bastards she had hopefully left behind. But time wasn't on her side, and sleep was only a prayer.

She dragged herself to her hands and knees and forced her body to move. Just a little farther, she promised herself. She shuddered as a leaf raked her nipple. Oh hell, it felt too good. Too damned good. Her nipples were hard points of exquisite sensation with no hope of relief. She knew well that no amount of touching them, of stroking her straining clit would bring anything more than an increase in arousal.

"Going somewhere, Charity?" She froze. Still on hands and knees, her eyes widened as a pair of boots and long muscular legs came into view.

Her gaze lifted. Up, over the shadowed expanse of tight thighs, a hard abdomen, a wide chest. His face was dark, his silver-gray eyes hidden, but she knew that voice. Knew his voice, and God help her, his scent. Rich and wild, with a hint of summer heat.

"Excuse me. Girls night out," she gasped as her womb shuddered again, peaking with pain, as though his scent called to her arousal.

She fought to change course, knowing she was caught, knowing there was no hope. He moved to counter her.

"You're in heat," he growled. She heard the fury throbbing in his voice and remembered his last vow to her. She shivered in dread.

She leaned against the thick trunk of a tree, sitting down wearily. She knew she was going into shock. She held her hand to her abdomen, feeling the blood that eased past the incision. She didn't bother to answer his accusation. There was no denying her arousal, or her depleted strength.

"So sue me." She leaned her head against the tree, watching as he hunched down in front of her, his body so tempting that if she had the strength she would have attacked him then and there. "Go away, I don't need your help."

She needed his cock. There was a difference. Hard, thick and long. She whimpered as she felt her cunt pulse more of her thick juices to her thighs. Glory be, she needed to be fucked. She hated the thought of dying, so aroused, unsatisfied.

"Was I offering to help you?" he asked her, his voice a bit too casual and light. Then he paused. She watched his head tilt, heard him inhale roughly. "Charity, you're bleeding." His voice had changed, edged with reluctant concern.

"I'm dying, Aiden," she whispered then, sadly. She would never know his touch, never know satisfaction.

She heard his indrawn breath, and wondered how he could smell the blood over the scent of raging lust.

"Not yet, you're not," he bit out, moving so quickly she could only cry out as he swung her into his arms, against the hard warmth of his chest. "You won't escape me that easily, Charity."

God, his body was hard, hot. One arm looped around his neck, the other pressed to her abdomen as she fought to stem the blood welling from the wound there.

She inhaled his scent, so wild and clean, as her breast brushed against the fabric of his shirt.

"I need you," she whimpered against his neck, the painful lust overcoming common sense or any shred of modesty.

She was naked in his arms, and he was hot and aroused. She could smell his arousal as well. A stormy, primal scent that wrapped around her, edging her own lusts higher.

"And you will have me," he grunted. "Sooner than you know. But not while you are bleeding to your death."

"You owe me," she cried out bleakly. "You do, Aiden. You owe me. Please make it stop hurting."

His arms tightened around her, his pace increasing as she moved against his chest. She was in need. The lightning flashes of aroused pain were torturous, worse than they had ever been before.

"Soon, Charity." His answer was a breath of sound. A promise or a warning? She wondered. "Sooner than either one of us needs."

He was striding through the jungle, moving at a rapid pace, holding her snugly to him, sharing his heat, his strength. Beneath her hand the blood flowed from her body. She could feel the chilling weakness washing over her and knew that this time she would not survive the loss of blood. She had lost too much, and the transfusions took too long for her body to accept. She would escape in death. What he had sought so many years before had now come to her.

"Can I sleep now, Aiden? I'm very tired," she asked him faintly as she felt the weakness closing over her.

She heard him curse. The sound was dark, deadly. The scientists had once again stolen what he believed was his. First his control, and now his vengeance.

She allowed her head to fall to his chest, a smile to shape her lips. And on a silent breath she whispered goodbye as darkness stole over her.

Chapter Two

ဆ

"She's your mate, she can only accept your blood." The doctor hastily prepared for the transfusion as her assistant stitched the incision on Charity's abdomen.

The pale skin was smeared with blood, too much blood. It had run in slow rivulets down her abdomen, smearing her thighs, and the smooth bare flesh between them. He had felt her weakening seconds before he reached camp, felt the fight that had always been so much a part of her slowly drain from her fragile body and knew he was losing her. She was dying in his arms.

His jaw bunched as he fought the anger surging through him. He turned his face from her, staring at the side of the tent that held the field hospital. If he watched her, looked at her lying there so pale and helpless, he didn't know if he would be able to contain his rage.

He had been warned of what was to come, though he had given little credence to the Breeds' declaration of psychic abilities to the point they claimed to possess them. He had scoffed at their knowledge of the bonds he knew would exist between them. Had mocked their predictions of the events to come. He had assured himself that night in the Labs had been due to the drugs, nothing more. Even though some internal sense had warned him otherwise.

He had been prepared to treat her as coldly, as cruelly as he would any Council lapdog. But the moment he had caught her scent, had seen her face, so pale, so distressed, he had been unable to maintain his determination. Her scent called out to him, her delicacy terrified him. She was so tiny now; so fragile he wondered how she had managed to escape on her own. She appeared too weak to even stand under her own strength, let alone to have escaped into the jungle.

He was within seconds of destroying every Council soldier and scientist they had taken, rather than holding them for questioning later by the Breed lawyers and government officials heading for the area. Remembering the smell of blood, of her impending death was nearly more than he could stand. They had done this to her. They had stripped her of all dignity and used her for their insane experiments. They had nearly killed her in their drive to play God.

He didn't stop to question his conflicting feelings regarding Charity. His fury over her betrayal of him, his hatred that she had stayed with the Council rather than fighting to be free. His desire for her, his fury at her. It all converged inside him until the morass of emotions became overpowering.

"Stop growling at me, Aiden," the doctor bit out nervously, her dark face watching him intently. "It doesn't hurt. It's just a needle."

She inserted said needle into the vein, opening the valve to allow his blood to ease gently through the tube that connected him to Charity. He didn't care about the damned needle. Over the course of his lifetime he had seen more needles than he could count.

"She's not my mate," he snarled, unable to hold the words back any longer. He knew the lie for what it was, though. "I have not accepted this."

The doctor snorted. She was young for her remarkable skill in Breed medicine. A bit on the short side, with full breasts and hips most men would ache to clasp close. Her skin was as pretty as milk chocolate, and she had long, sleek black hair that fell down her back in a multitude of braids.

"Her body says otherwise." She crossed her arms beneath her breasts as she stared down at him, glancing often at the speed of the transfusion. "You can't deny the mating, Aiden. You know that."

He looked up at her broodingly. She watched him as she would a recalcitrant child. The forced patience and mocking amusement had him baring his teeth in warning.

"I can deny whatever I wish," he snapped. "I did not mark her. How can she be my mate?"

She frowned at the question. Her studies into the mating phenomena that began with Hope were well known. She was determined to learn why the Feline Breeds had bred so easily, whereas the Wolf Breeds had been unable to. The scientists had theorized for years that the inability to breed could reverse. It had been proven with the Feline Pride. The Wolf Packs had not yet accomplished that last battle with nature, though.

"If what I suspect is true when she swallowed your semen in that Lab six years ago, that was all it took. I suspected the mating could occur without the mark, and this proves it. The blood tests don't lie, Aiden. Her body is bound to yours. The hormone and unique DNA that marks it matches yours perfectly. The enzyme in her blood that rejects any other transfusion further proves it. Deny it all you like, but she's a part of you."

Aiden refused to answer the charge. His blood boiled at the thought of being tied to this woman. Any woman. The life of a Breed was too dangerous. The life of a Breed mate was even more so. The low, vicious growl that rumbled in his throat couldn't be silenced. The silent disapproval of his conscience was just as loud.

Had it not been for Keegan warning them that her body would accept no other blood but Aiden's, they would have lost her. Not that Dr. Armani hadn't run the first vital testing for blood match. She had run the tests as her assistant prepped Charity for the transfusion. Each second had seemed a lifetime as she bled uncontrollably.

"How much longer will this take?" He flicked a contemptuous glance at the blood-filled tube that led from his arm. "I have work to do."

The scent of her need, even unconscious, was destroying him. Sweet and tempting, the subtle fragrance stirred him, keeping his cock engorged, his body ready to take her. He hated the uncontrolled response. The need, as hard and brutal as it had been while the drugs pumped through his system years before.

"She is more important," she informed him, her voice turning cold.

Aiden lifted his lip contemptuously. To the doctor, she might be more important. To the Wolf Breeds she might be more important. To him, she was the enemy, he assured himself. He would not let his unruly body sway him where she was concerned. She had worked with the Council for years now, been a part of their inner workings, knew their secrets and their evil. Even when she could have escaped them, she stayed. Working with them rather than fighting to be free.

No sane person could have spent so many years in the bosom of such monsters and not be like them. The denial that clawed in his heart for so many years refused to accept this, but Aiden knew it was no more than the truth. He would not be led by his emotions in this.

Charity was a Council doctor, one of their most valued Lab Technicians and budding scientists, and yet none of them saw the potential of betrayal here.

"All done." Dr. Nicole Armani's voice was soft, yet tinged with disapproval as she removed the transfusion catheter. "You can return to whatever you deem important now, Aiden."

He rose slowly to his feet.

"How long will she be unconscious?" He prided himself on his control then. He stood before the doctor, careless, unconcerned.

"I don't know, Aiden." She shook her head, watching as the assistant worked over Charity. "She's lost a lot of blood, her body was in shock from whatever drugs they had pumped into her, and she was already weakened. It could be hours, it could be days."

He flexed his fist carefully. "I'll have one of my men stationed as guard. If she awakens, call for me. If not, she will be leaving on the air transport coming in this evening."

"Aiden, she's too weak." Dr. Armani turned on him in angry surprise. "She may not survive the trip. She needs to be stabilized further."

His mouth opened to snap at her, to reinforce the order, but his gaze was caught by the silent, too pale woman on the bed. He wanted to howl at himself in rage as an unfamiliar weakness rose inside him. She was too pale. Too weak. He wanted her away from here, yet he couldn't endanger her further. Some instinct he couldn't deny or fight refused to allow him to test her fragile strength.

"When?" His voice was a harsh, contained growl of fury.

"Not before she stabilizes," Armani said again, her voice stubborn. "A day, a week, whatever. I'll let you know when she can be moved."

Frustration bit at him with sharp, hungry teeth. Charity would soon be in more danger by staying here than she would be if she were moved too early. The implication of her health and the war raging through the jungle with the escaped Council soldiers and Coyotes was a difficult problem. One he needed to resolve quickly.

"We have limited time here." He gnashed his teeth together, frustration mounting inside him.

"Aiden, do you want her to die?" She turned on him then, facing him with a frown, her black eyes glittering angrily. "It's my job to keep her alive. Period. Do you think I don't know what I'm doing? I will let you know the minute I think she can be moved. If all goes well, possibly — and I stress *possibly* — tomorrow."

He raked his fingers through his hair in a burst of anger. "We may not have this time you need, Doctor," he bit out. "We must be cleared out of here as quickly as possible. You are aware of this, I assume?" He sneered the question at her.

They couldn't afford an organized assault by soldiers possibly on their way to free those taken captive. The war between the Council and the Breeds was heating up in ways that left him struggling for the answer to their survival.

Dr. Armani drew herself stiffly erect. Her brows lowered dangerously, a tight smile shaping her lips. "Don't push me, Aiden. I am not one of your Enforcers and I won't be ordered about. You take care of your responsibilities and I will care of mine. We'll both live that way." She was beginning to appear decidedly violent.

"Are you threatening me, Armani?" he questioned her then, dangerously. No one had dared threaten him since the day they escaped the Labs.

"Sounds like she is, Aiden." Faith stepped into the tent, dirt-smudged, and frowning in concern. "We need you outside. Jacob and Wolfe just pulled in the head scientist. It's Robertson, and he's ready to talk."

Robertson. Dr. Andrew Robertson, second only to Bainesmith, before her death. He would now be considered the Council's top expert in Breed experimentation. Aiden smiled coldly. He glanced back at Charity, promising himself that she would awaken soon, and when she did, she would not escape him or his vengeance.

"Were they able to retrieve any of the records?" he asked her quickly, forcing his mind away from Charity and her fragile health. "We need those records, Faith."

She shook her head as they rushed from the tent. "Nothing, Aiden. Keegan was able to get into the records room before the explosion. Let's pray they were destroyed. From what I've seen, we don't want to know what happened here."

He heard her compassion, her pain. And in many ways he agreed with her. The Lab had been hell, the smell of death and depravity nearly strangling them as they entered it. They had enough nightmares. God knew they didn't need anymore.

"Let's go see if we can choke some facts out of him then," he smiled mercilessly. "I'm in the mood to be persuasive."

Chapter Three

ℬ

He was in the mood to be sick. Aiden stood inside the jungle, just out of sight of camp and fought to breathe. It wasn't the sickness in his gut that caused the problems though, it was the emotional turmoil pitching through his soul. He wiped at his damp face and assured himself it was the heat of the night, not tears that dampened his face.

Propping his arm against the tree beside him he buried his face against it, his muscles taut from the tension riding his body. God help him, he wanted to kill them all. There were twenty-five soldiers and nearly a dozen scientists restrained within the tent he had just left and he wanted to rip their throats out. He wanted to hear their screams of pain, see them on their knees begging him a second before he tasted their blood.

His fists clenched in driving fury as he stood there, fighting to control his breathing, his rage.

> We tied her down. The hormone had to be inserted directly into the womb with the ability to view the resulting changes. We decided rather than going in through the cervix, that it would be easier to make the incision into the womb itself and insert the camera probe directly inside.

Easier for them. The growl that rumbled in his throat was a primal protest to the claim. It was no easier. It was more painful. It was a shock to the body when none was needed, and she had nearly bled to death more than once in the process.

Included in the experiments was a hormonal aphrodisiac made from the hormone in his semen. The arousal it produced was found to have stimulated the ovaries in some way. They were merely awaiting a new ovulation period before attempting to force conception with the few remaining samples they had of his sperm. They had been certain the changes within her womb would allow conception to occur.

Her records had revealed the ingestion of his semen. They had found the perfect specimen for yet more of their monstrous tests. For six months. Six agonizing months where she had wasted away to nothing, driven closer and closer to the brink of death.

And had she died, they would have tossed her body away as yet another broken specimen. She wouldn't have mattered, only the results of the tests did. Tests that stripped the mind and horrified the soul. He was still reeling from the reports the guards and lower level scientists were more than eager to give in exchange for their lives.

"She lives. This should be all that matters." He raised his head, staring at the Winged Breed they had been forced to drag from the flames of the Lab as he fought to return and save the woman he knew was still held there.

Keegan was nearly six and a half feet tall though lacking the heavy muscle that most Breeds developed. Not that he appeared weak. He stood tall, his arms crossed over his chest, aristocratic and graceful. His long brown hair fell past his shoulders, his amber eyes were intent and focused.

Aiden shook his head. He still couldn't believe they had managed to do it. They had given man wings. Full, strong, graceful wings that folded upon his back. They extended from his boot-shod feet to the top of his head with nearly an eighteen foot wing span to hold his human body within the sky. The bone work of the Winged Breeds was less dense and more flexible than those of full-humans and other Breeds. He was a miracle of genetic perfection, and psychic to boot. Son of a bitch, if he wouldn't be a pain in the ass.

"I should kill every damned scientist sitting in that tent," Aiden growled. "Eventually they'll be released, just as the other bastards were six years before. It will never stop, Keegan."

The knowledge that there was little he could to stop the madness ate at him, just as it always had. The experiments still continued and the Council cruelties seemed to only magnify each time another Lab was found. There was no mercy, no humanity in the men and women who ran those Labs. Only the experiment mattered.

The wings at Keegan's back shifted as though in agitation. He breathed in deeply, his gaze rising to the sheltering branches overhead before his eyes returned to Aiden's.

"It seems very hopeless I know," he sighed. "But I do not believe it will always be so, Aiden. I believe the new future, desperate though it may be at times, will make a way for us all. We must prepare our children for that day. Keep them strong enough to lead. Strong enough to survive."

As though the Breeds needed children to worry about as well. Innocent lives thrown smack in the middle of a scientific war on humanity versus the lack of. And as Keegan hinted, victory would be a long way down the futuristic road.

Aiden grunted. "Yeah, I figured I could forget ever seeing it myself."

He wiped a hand over his face before spearing his fingers restlessly through his hair. Regaining his control was a battle this time. This Lab, the tests that had been described to him, were too horrific for him to accept.

"A day will come when it will end. But it is yet far off," Keegan finally shrugged. "Nature has smiled on us, though. She has found us worthy of life, and of continuing. Your mate will prove this to the world. Your son will help lead in a future race to triumph. We can do nothing but pave the way for him and the others that shall follow."

Mate. His teeth snapped together at the word. His mate and his child. He ignored the flare of heat in his cock, fought back the instinctive possessive instincts and snarled violently.

"I do not accept this woman as my mate," he bit out.

A chuckle echoed in the darkness. Keegan's laughter. His superior attitude was beginning to grate on Aiden's nerves.

"Nature has done this for you," Keegan informed him with no small amount of amusement. "Perhaps she knew you were not worthy to choose. Often pride and our human frailties will hide the truth from our eyes until our mistakes are too excessive, have caused too much damage to ever set right. So she has instead given such choices to the animal that resides in us, to recognize our other half. The one created exclusively for us."

Aiden snorted. "There are, at last count, five women for every male out in the world..."

"There is at present less than a dozen female Breeds from all those created. There are over six hundred known Breed males, and perhaps more unknown."

Shock widened Aiden's eyes. "Three hundred," he bit out. "Last count is three hundred."

"Ah." Keegan nodded. "Over six hundred known to me then. My count is of course more accurate I can assure you. But that is neither here nor there. Humans are naturally predisposed to female children. It will not be so for Breeds, who will be predisposed to males. What would you make of this, Aiden?"

Shit. He bit back a stream of curses at the information. Not that he wholly trusted the Winged male's knowledge. Unfortunately, he suspected the man knew exactly what he was talking about. Which only complicated things further.

"More trouble than we need," he sighed roughly. "Our males will mate with full-human females. The Purists that will arise will go crazy."

"Yes." Keegan nodded slowly. "But not more than the Breeds can manage."

He would have said more, Aiden thought, if one of the Enforcers hadn't chosen that moment to call his out his name as he approached them.

"Aiden, Armani needs you back at the tent. The girl is bleeding again and she's frightened she may need another transfusion."

He flinched, turning back to Keegan with a flash of worry.

"Her life is in your hands, Aiden," he said softly. "It is your choice now if she lives or dies. Now is the time to make it."

Aiden narrowed his eyes in frustrated fury. "You know, Keegan, I could grow to hate you," he snarled. "Quite easily."

He didn't give the Winged Breed a chance to respond. He turned and rushed back to the camp, heading for the medical tent and the woman, Nature, in all her supposed wisdom, decided was his mate.

* * * * *

"And I could grow to hate you as well, Aiden, quite easily," Keegan murmured as he watched the other Breed rush from the darkness toward the well camp.

"Is this not the way of all alphas?" a soft voice asked him with gentle amusement, touching his mind with a light, feminine touch.

He snorted. *"There are alphas and then there are fools. Which, I wonder, will he ultimately be?"*

"You have not seen this yet?" the voice asked softly. *"It must be because you have refused to look."*

He shrugged defiantly, as though the voice could see such a movement. *"I would prefer not to regret what I can not change."*

He had a fondness for Charity. Not a love, or a jealousy of what Aiden possessed, but a fondness. Her soul was gentle, her heart filled with warmth. She was the only human he had met who possessed such qualities.

"And if you do not look, how do you know it cannot be changed?" the voice asked.

He sighed wearily. "*Are there not duties for you to attend to? Surely wherever you are, there are things you must do other than harass me.*"

"*Actually, my duty is to harass you more often.*" Her laughter filled his mind. "*I have been accused of being quite lazy where you are concerned.*"

"*Who would dare?*" he mocked her patiently then.

She laughed again. A whispery little chuckle that tempted him to smile.

"*Will you be leaving there soon?*" she asked.

"Within the hour. We are preparing to fly now. They will be upset at our absence."

"*There are things you must do, Keegan. They will survive without your knowledge. Remember, what comes easy is not near as important as those things you must fight for.*"

And there was much, he thought, left to fight for. Shaking his head at the cruelties of man and the fickleness of fate, he moved farther into the jungle for the clearing he had landed in earlier. Unfurling his wings he lifted them to the breeze coming behind him and took a running leap into flight.

Charity would suffer for the desertion, but he had seen enough to know that her trials were those she must face alone. He had his own destiny to conquer, his own trials to endure. And it must all begin now.

Chapter Four
Breed Compound
Colorado Mountains

Charity came awake with a moan of pain. How she had managed to sleep, to escape the blinding pain of the drugs, she wasn't certain. How she came awake in the unfamiliar room was even more confusing. She blinked weakly up at the rough beamed ceiling wondering where she was, what had happened.

A spasm of convulsive reaction shook her womb, taking her breath, as she moaned harshly. She could feel the dampness between her thighs, the ever-present arousal that spiked through her body. The sexual need she could tolerate, she had learned to accept it over the years. It was the blinding pain of the attempts at forced fertility that weakened her mind.

When the contractive shudder eased away she looked around the room. The bedroom was large and almost homey. On the other side of the room an open fireplace burned cheerily, the flames warming the rooms with heated comfort. The bed was canopied, the thick flannel curtains tied back along the rough wood posts. Several comfortable chairs sat on the other side of the room, beside a large chest and dresser.

To her side a door was open to another room, obviously a bathroom. Thank God, she needed one. She checked carefully, she wasn't restrained in any way. Her wrists weren't sore, though her feet felt like hell. She pushed the quilts from her body, finally realizing she was dressed in a large T-shirt, but nothing else. She wasn't going to bitch; she hadn't been allowed to wear clothes in six months.

She moved weakly to the side of the bed, biting her lip at the pain in her legs and ankles as she swung them from the bed. She dreaded putting any weight on her feet. She could feel their tenderness, the pain awaiting her.

She bit off her cry of agony as she gingerly stood up. Tears filled her eyes and within moments dampened her cheeks as she shuffled to the small room. Once there, she used the toilet, washed her hands and face and glanced longingly at the tub before shaking her head. If she got in, she would never pull herself out.

As she washed her face, she found a clean toothbrush still within its box and worked it free quickly. She felt almost freshened after brushing her teeth and forced herself back to the bed. Her breaths were panting whimpers by the time she sat down on the mattress and managed to pull her legs onto the bed.

She collapsed across it, breathing heavily, trying to relax through the contractions in her abdomen. She felt along the incision, surprised that no blood was leaking free. It was bandaged, obviously stitched closed. She blinked in confusion toward the fireplace, trying to remember, to understand the abrupt changes around her.

No cells, no scientists, no restraints. She breathed in deeply, knowing there was something she had forgotten, something she needed to remember. Shadowed images flickered through her mind. Flames and fear, a blinding heat as she fought to escape. She shook her head, trying to make sense of it.

"You shouldn't be out of bed. If you had called I would have helped you."

Fear shocked her system. The breath lodged in her throat as she stared unblinkingly at the fire, trying to deny the voice that had spoken. It wasn't possible, she assured herself. Not now. Not after all these years.

His voice was colder than it had been in the Mexican Labs. More savage and controlled than she remembered. She licked her lips nervously, wondering if she would survive the savagery she glimpsed in his eyes.

"You can't ignore me forever, Charity." Smooth, mocking amusement raked across her nerves as leanly muscled thighs came into her line of vision. Between the jean-clad columns, a thick, hard erection bulged against the snug, low-slung cloth.

Charity swallowed in tight reaction as her nipples peaked, hardening with increased arousal. She fought to breathe through the welcoming shudders in her womb. As though her body had instinctively recognized its sexual master, it began to hum in joy. A joy her mind rejected, the intellectual part of her aware that she may have well escaped the physical pain, but the emotional agony to come could well be worse.

Muscles flexed, his abdomen tightened as he bent his knees, lowering himself until he could stare at her from the bottom of the bed. Her breath hitched in her throat. He was older, his features honed, harder. His eyes were a silver-gray, merciless, as cold as ice.

Black hair fell shaggy and thick around his face as he propped his forearms on the mattress, watching her silently. Satisfaction lined his expression, tormenting, knowing.

"Well," she cleared her throat weakly. "Out of the frying pan and into the fire." She commented on her apparent rescue from the Labs, only to find herself now held by the one man she had fought to escape for years.

A thick black brow arched questioningly. "An interesting analogy. Would you like me to contact the Council and return you?"

She flinched. He would, she thought, and likely do so gladly. But which was really worse?

"How did you find me? Did you find the Winged Breeds as well?" she finally bit out when she couldn't answer her own question. The pain in her womb only fed her anger, fed her sense of desperation.

His expression darkened. "We found them. Do you remember the attack at all? Your escape from the Labs?"

Escape? There had been no rescue? She forced herself to shake her head negatively. "What happened?" Not that she cared at this point. She was free of them, and she would die before going back.

"You somehow managed to escape just before the explosion brought the mountain down. We had already rescued Keegan and the others, but had been unable to get to you. I found you afterwards, nearly unconscious in the jungle." He watched her closely. The look was so intent she dropped her own gaze.

"How did you find me?" Shards of memory flashed through her mind, making more sense as the seconds passed.

"Keegan led me to you." His voice was calm, holding little, if any, emotion. The very fact that he appeared so emotionless was more frightening than his anger could have been.

"He should have left me to die," she grunted sarcastically. "It would have been far kinder."

"Not to mention less complicated." Aiden surged to his feet, causing her to flinch in dizzied reaction. "Our doctor has examined you and found no lasting injuries. You've been washed, disinfected and stitched. You should be well soon."

Disinfected. Morbid amusement filled her. As though she had somehow been contagious. She closed her eyes, fighting the overwhelming futility of fighting further. Unfortunately, something inside her refused to allow her to give in. A spark of rage, of anger. Not just at the Council, but at Aiden as well. Had it not been for him and his determination to die too soon, she wouldn't be in this mess right now.

"Thank you for the update," she gritted out as she closed her eyes, fighting to breathe through the surging contractions in her abdomen. If he would just go the hell away then she could be miserable in peace.

She heard him sigh roughly. "I can smell the scent of your arousal. You're horny, Charity." His voice was edged with frustration.

"Poor me," she sniped as she gritted her teeth against the pain.

"The scent offends me." He sounded angry, as though she expected him to relieve the pain.

"Poor you." She wasn't about to ask him for anything, even if it was his damned fault. "If it offends you so damned bad then get the hell away from me!" She shot him a look that she hoped showed her rising fury. Like she needed a damned update concerning the state of her own body.

She tensed then as a particularly agonizing bolt of pain tore through her womb. It was getting worse. She fought to control the scream building in her throat, but couldn't stop the whimper that escaped her lips. Before she could do more than gasp, Aiden flipped her to her back, holding her down, increasing the pain that radiated like a cascade of fireworks through her body.

"Stop," she wheezed, desperate to curl back into the fetal position she had assumed when the pain first started.

She could feel the cold sweat breaking out on her face, the screams building in her throat. She hated being this weak in front of him, in such pain she was helpless against whatever cruelty he would inflict.

"Do you think you can go on hurting like this?" His question was a hard, rough growl. "The pain is killing you, Charity."

"Saves you the trouble," she cried out furiously, fighting her need to arch to him, to rub against him. God, he was heavy and hard against her, and she needed him so desperately. Alternately, fury whipped at the edges of her mind. He was being less than considerate of a condition that was basically his fault. His next words exploded through her, though, searing past the arousal to an anger bordering on rage.

"Beg me and I'll ease you." She glimpsed the cold smile on his face, the flash of his canines.

Finally, mercifully, the pain eased again until she could breathe normally and felt less like vomiting in his face. Bastard, he would have deserved it.

"Fuck you, Aiden," she snarled.

She brought her knee up fast, not overly hard as the pain left her weak and dazed, but hard enough. His eyes widened as he paled before falling to his side with a groan of pain, his hands going instinctively to his offended cock.

Knowing retaliation would be quick, she tried to roll from the bed, to crawl from him. She couldn't believe she had struck out. Couldn't believe she had actually done it. Amusement flashed through her for a second as she remembered the look of horror on his face before a growl of animal fury sounded behind her.

Chapter Five

ॐ

Pain was pain, she thought, as he gripped her shoulders and jerked her back to the bed. The constant flashes of fire through her body were worse than anything he could inflict on her, short of broken bones.

He came over her, his knees a vice about her legs as he stared down at her with dark, icy calm. She knew she was supposed to be frightened of his anger; she could see it in his eyes, feel it in the waves of fury emanating from him. His assurance that she would cower beneath his rage was there in his self-satisfied expression.

"I won't beg you, and I won't cower before you," she bit out, her teeth gritting as her muscles tightened again in defense of the pain that struck her womb.

She was shaking, perspiration coating her skin as she fought her tears. And Aiden was only making it worse. The touch of his body, his weight holding her down, his hands warm and calloused as he held her wrists above her head, combined to increase her arousal and in return the fiery waves of hunger that swept over her. The pain was brutal, like a fist punch to the gut as her womb spasmed in need.

"You're so desperate to be fucked that your whole body screams out for it," he sneered. "You'll beg soon."

"Not to you," she snarled back. "I'd rather fuck a mongrel Coyote than ask you for anything, Aiden. Bastard that you are, you'd leave me hurting anyway."

He narrowed his eyes as the corner of his upper lip lifted, showing the sharp canine in deadly relief. As though the sight of it frightened her. She would have snorted if she could find the breath to push that much air through her body at one time.

"You will go to no other," he bit out. "When you decide to ask me nicely for relief, Charity, perhaps I will be nice and extend it."

He jumped from her then, staring down at her, breathing hard and rough as he watched her. Her eyes went down his body, until her gaze locked on the thick bulge beneath his jeans.

"You're horny too, Aiden," she said softly. "Maybe you need to beg me. Ask me politely for relief and perhaps I will extend it."

She gasped then as a particularly hard contraction tightened her abdomen. She curled quickly on her side, fighting the waves of pain as she felt more of her juices leak from between her thighs.

"Damn you!" she cursed him breathlessly. "It's your fault. You did this to me, and you hate me for saving your miserable life. Bastard."

"Is that what you believe, Charity?" He leaned close to her, his teeth bared in his own anger. "That I hate you? I do not hate you, darling, for saving me. I hate you for tying me to you. For taking my choice and my will from me. But more than anything else, I will never forgive you for betraying me as you did, and leaving me helpless in that bitch's hands. That I won't forgive you for."

* * * * *

Aiden stalked from the bedroom, unable to look at her, to smell the sweet scent of her need. She was his mate. He hadn't truly believed it, had paid little heed to Cian's claims in the weeks before they attacked the Labs. He hadn't truly believed. He believed now. Had believed before bringing her to his home. But that didn't mean he had to like it. It didn't mean he couldn't fight it.

He pushed his fingers restlessly through his hair as he heard her moan again. Every muscle in his body tightened in agony. The blood burned in his veins, seared his cock. He ached for her, like nothing he had ever known in his life. And he knew he wouldn't deny her much longer.

He moved to the stove where a pot of stew bubbled merrily. She had to eat. She was too thin, too weakened to carry a child if she did conceive as Cian had said she would. Right now, he doubted if she could even withstand his lust or the sexual intensity that would come from their mating. What terrified him the most, though, was wondering if she would survive how his body would lock with hers, ensuring his seed every chance to find root within her body.

He heard her moan again. A bleak, pain-ridden sound that tore at his soul. Damn her. He flipped the stove off, setting the pot to a back burner as he flipped the cooking spoon into the sunlit sink. His cock was heavy, fully erect, confined behind the material of his jeans and begging for release. Arousal had never fired his blood with such a firestorm of hunger.

He remembered the day she had coaxed his erection to bursting relief. After taking his first release into her mouth, she had followed Bainesmith's orders and left the Labs. It was then his hell had truly begun.

Hard, aching for her, his cock had stayed erect, desperate for relief. With mouth and hands, Bainesmith had drained him more than once into her fucking vials for testing. For hours, until he hung limply on that fucking metal cross, sweat dripping from his body as they put his unwilling arousal to hard use.

And he had fucked. Just as they wanted. When they wheeled the unknown woman's gurney to him, adjusted her to allow the penetration into the hot depths of her pussy, he had fucked her. And fucked her. And still he had not eased. Bainesmith had been more than pleased.

Thankfully though, after the first time Charity had sucked the seed from his body, the further swelling in his thick shaft had not occurred. The fist-sized knot had stayed silent, though he could feel its need just beneath his desperate flesh.

When he was finally returned to his cell, his body thick with sweat, his cock coated with the woman's sap and his own seed, he could do nothing but collapse onto his cot and swear his vengeance. On Bainesmith and on Charity.

But how do you reap vengeance when it's your mate?

She cried out again, the sound low, tortured. She was in need. Her body hot and pulsing, pleading silently with him to fill it. The drugs injected into her pushed her natural arousal higher; those injected into her womb increased her fertility. She would carry his child.

His hands trembled as his cock throbbed to the point that he was forced to grip it in defense. He bared his teeth in helplessness. She was his. His mate. And by God, now was as good a time as any to prove it.

Chapter Six

ဆာ

"Do you know what will happen when I take you?"
Charity opened her eyes in surprise as Aiden moved to the
end of the bed.

Her eyes widened as his shirt drifted to the floor and his
hands went to the worn leather belt threaded through the
loops of his jeans. Her mouth watered. She could almost sense
the hot male taste of his thick, hard flesh. She remembered it
clearly, relived it often in her dreams.

"You haven't asked me politely yet," she reminded him,
trying to snarl then wincing at the thick arousal in her voice.
As though he had to ask. She knew when he touched her she
would go off like skyrockets.

Her breasts ached now, her nipples feeling more swollen,
if that were possible, than ever before.

He released the metal buttons on his jeans, one by one, as
her breathing increased.

"Do you know what will happen, Charity?" he asked her
again. The heavy warning in his voice had her swallowing
tightly with nerves and shades of fear.

"I know the basics," she bit out. "I'm not stupid. And I'm
not ready to fuck you yet, either. Beg me, Aiden." Her womb
clenched in protest.

His hands paused. The jeans were undone, yet still
covering him.

"You know the basics of Wolf Breed sex?' he asked her
carefully. "You know how I'll lock inside you?"

She remembered then, the hard knot she had barely kept
hidden from the scientists as Aiden shot his seed into her

mouth. She trembled, her eyes widening as she stared up at him. Like an animal, he would lock inside her, ensuring his seed had time to reach her fertile womb.

She moaned bleakly. Her eyes closed as she fought the knowledge of what was to come. Now she understood the reasons behind the careful blood tests the scientists had conducted, trying to match her blood to one of the Coyote Breeds stationed there. Looking for a match. A breeding pair. An animal that would lock inside her.

"Don't touch me." She jerked away from him as she felt his touch at her shoulder. "Get the hell away from me, damn you."

She scrambled to the headboard of the bed, refusing to look at him. She fought to ignore the pleading ache in her body, the arousal that only seemed to grow. How the hell was she supposed to bear this if he touched her?

"The pain is killing you, Charity," he said softly.

Her gaze flickered to him, then away, as he shed his jeans. She shuddered. She knew how thick and hard his cock was, and knew how desperately her body needed it. Her body, her heart, but not her mind. She wasn't a breeding vessel.

"Aiden, I can't do this." She shook her head desperately. "Please, please leave me alone. The pain will go away…"

"I remember a time when I begged you similarly," he reminded her coolly. "Do you remember that time, Charity? Yet, you sucked me to my release regardless, and then left me to suffer the agony of needing only your body, and being forced to accept the alternative."

"At least you were fucking instead of bleeding to death," she snapped, staring at him, enraged. "If death is so preferable to you, no one is stopping you now. Want me to help you load the gun?"

He moved up on the bed, crawling to her, his eyes a cold, hard gray as he watched her.

"I fucked for them, Charity," he growled viciously as though she hadn't spoken at all. "For hours. I could not get enough, could not come enough. I screwed every hole I was given access to that night, and still my cock would not soften. Now, you will relieve that ache, Charity. The ache that has lingered ever since that cursed day."

He was furious because she had saved his miserable life? She gritted her teeth in fury. Why was she surprised? For some reason she had thought over the years that he would have seen the good sense behind such a move. But oh no, not Aiden. She should have known it was too much to hope for.

"They would have killed you." She slapped at his hand as he touched the hem of the shirt she wore. "I couldn't let you die then, but by God you can go to hell now." She glared at him, trembling with anger and need.

"And now, I will not let you die." The material shredded beneath his hands. From hem to neck, then down the back as he tore the cloth as easily as paper.

She cried out, struggling against him as she fought to get away from him, to resist the scent of him, the touch that beckoned and made her body plead for more.

"Easy, Charity." He caught her close as she fought to jerk away from him.

He was warm. She shivered with the need to burrow closer. Oh God, his body was so warm it seemed to sink into that hidden, frozen core of her soul that never seemed to melt.

"Let me hold you for a moment." His arms tightened around her as she fought to breathe.

Her back was plastered to his chest, his arms holding hers clamped to her side, his hands flattening on the painfully clenched muscles of her abdomen. His fingers stroked the skin there, delicately massaging and easing the shuddering muscles.

"I only wanted to save you," she whispered as his heat seeped into her body. "I knew rescue was coming, Aiden. I

54

contacted that reporter and told him where the Lab was. I knew help would be there."

"You forced me to betray my body, my own instincts, Charity," he whispered in her ear, the sound dark and feral. "You were my mate, and you forced me to betray you. I gave your pleasure, and my seed to another. And you calmly walked away."

She shook her head desperately. "It wasn't like that." She wanted to stay angry, needed to, but her body was weak, worn and so aroused that the clenching of her cunt was more a spasmodic reaction to her overwhelming sexual hunger than a reflection of her mind's willingness to engage in the act.

His cock jerked at her back, hot and hard, a velvet stroke of power that further inflamed her body.

"I'm going to take you. I will take you as I see fit, as many times as I wish. Beginning now, Charity. Fighting me, fighting the need, will only make it worse. I know this from experience, mate."

He was still angry. His fury stroked her as casually as his hands massaged her abdomen, moving lower, closer every second to the wet heat of her cunt. She was on her knees, held close to him, helpless in his grip and her own needs.

"I can't wait to bury myself inside you." The growl in his voice shocked her with the sound of primal heat. "I feel as though my blood is boiling, Charity, demanding you, demanding your tight pussy wrapped around my cock."

She inhaled sharply. His voice was deep, pitched low, as he whispered at her ear, his breath stroking over the delicate shell with erotic heat. She wanted him, needed him so desperately that fighting against it seemed a useless task. Until she thought of the consequences.

"Aiden, wait." She shuddered as his lips feathered over her neck, then his teeth scraped the sensitive skin with a nip of barely restrained hunger.

"For what?" His hands stroked upward, his palms molding themselves to the full mounds of her breasts, his thumbs and forefingers capturing her peaked nipples.

Charity lost her breath, and her mind, in that instant. Her eyes closed as her head fell back against his broad shoulder and she pressed more firmly into the grip.

"Do you like that, Charity?" He pressed closer to her, his canines scraping across her shoulder with sensual promise.

His fingers worked her nipples slowly, with just enough pressure to further inflame the lusts building in her body. His palms cupped her with heated warmth, but his wicked fingers only stroked her internal fires higher, hotter. And all the while his lips, his tongue, the sharp points of his canines rasped at the skin of her neck and shoulder. She could feel her flesh tingling, pleading for a deeper caress.

"You're torturing me. Deliberately," she panted, her voice rough, trembling almost as badly as her body was.

"I've thought of this day for years," he growled at her ear. "Each time I took another woman and felt her pussy parting for me, taking me, I've thought of you, Charity. Thought of you, and wondered just how long it would take me to fuck you out of my system."

Shock tore through her body a second before she jerked out of his arms. Before he could stop her, she moved across the bed, biting off a cry of painful regret as she lost the heat of his body. She came to her knees, facing him, ignoring the jarring spasms in her womb.

He faced her. He didn't move to pull her back into his arms, or to touch her in any way. The smirk that lingered on his lips tempted her to violence, though. The heavy, bulging thickness of his cock tempted her in ways she didn't want to consider.

"I am not your mate," she rasped out. "The pain will go away. The need will become no more than an echo, and when I can walk, I'll show you just how fast I can remove myself from your pitiful life, Aiden. I want no part of you."

"Isn't that too bad," he snarled, his eyes darkening, muscles tensing with anger. "You won't leave, Charity. Not now, not ever. Mating is forever, baby."

"Is it?" She lifted a brow, knowing the sarcastic impression it would convey. "Drugs do not make a mate, Aiden."

"And all the denials in the world won't change the nature of the beast, Charity," he bit out. "Accept it or not. Your body will accept no blood but mine, your body longs for mine. The hormone driving you crazy is mine..."

"It's a drug," she cried out, spearing her fingers through her hair. "It's the damned drugs, Aiden. That's all."

He snorted mockingly as he moved from the bed.

"Drugs be damned, woman." He shot her a hot, angry glance. "Can you tell me you had no desire for me? That your body didn't melt daily in need? That your pussy didn't stay hot and wet for me after swallowing my sperm? Tell me it didn't. I dare you."

His superior expression, the sneering knowledge in his eyes, inflamed her. She lifted her chin, staring him in the eye as she watched him with a mocking twist of her lips.

"Of course I did, Aiden." She shrugged. "I didn't say you couldn't make me horny. I was as much a prisoner as you were. Of course I would have fucked you. You turned me on. That doesn't make me your mate. It doesn't make me any part of you. The drugs did that, not nature."

She watched his lips thin, his eyes narrow on her intently. As though he could see past her building fury, past her protestations. She wasn't about to tell him just how hot she did get in those years before she was caught betraying the Council. No more than she was about to tell him the results of the tests she had run on herself.

She watched as he breathed in hard and deep, his nostrils flaring as he fought for control. His expression was a study in sensuality. His lips looked just slightly fuller than normal, his bronzed skin flushed along the cheekbones. His chest, bare of hair, wide and muscular, tense with his effort to control his own raging lusts.

Finally, his lips quirked. Not mockingly, but with genuine amusement.

"When I can touch you, Charity, and your body doesn't heat with longing, your cunt doesn't cream with need, then we'll discuss whether it's the drugs or nature. Until then, you are my mate, whether it's what you wish or not."

"You're a bastard, Aiden." She clenched her teeth as she fought the building fury, the rush of blood that only stroked her arousal higher.

"Most likely," he agreed softly. "But for the moment, mate, I'm your bastard. Deal with that however you will."

Chapter Seven

ဆ

"Time to eat." Charity watched as Aiden moved slowly to the bed several hours later, his expression set in determined lines as he picked up a pair of long sweat pants from the chair by the bed and approached her. "Come on. I'll help you get dressed and carry you into the kitchen."

She shivered at the sound of his voice.

"I'm not hungry." She shook her head. Right now she was more concerned with keeping herself from jumping his broad body and stuffing his cock up her pussy. She felt like a rabid animal, intent on mating.

"You look hungry." He frowned down at her.

Oh, he had no idea.

"I'm fine," she gritted out.

"You don't look fine," he pointed out a little too patiently to suit her.

She opened her eyes, staring up at him with a lack of amusement or patience.

"I look like a scrawny bitch in heat, which is pretty much what I am," she said with blistering emphasis. "So go away and let me die in peace."

Aiden sighed patiently, the sound further grating on her nerves. He held out the pants. "Dress willingly or I can force them on you. Your choice, Charity."

She knew she needed to eat. Knew she needed to regain her strength but the blistering arousal tormenting her was unlike anything she had known previously. The pain wasn't nearly as blinding as the need to be touched. But if he touched her, if he took her, she knew the consequences could be catastrophic.

Gathering her strength and her courage, she sat up slowly, watching him warily as she held out her hand for the pants. He ignored her. He knelt at her feet with a warning look. Likely daring her not to kick his teeth in, she thought with a hidden smile. Oh, how satisfying that would be.

Aiden hid his grin as he watched her. Her expression didn't change, but the forced curve of her mouth, the stillness about her cheekbones warned him. He remembered in a flash of insight seeing that look on her face a second before she nearly ripped the balls off one of the Lab guards years before. Patient, calm. Exacting.

He eased the material over her legs, watching them carefully for any tensing. He would need only a second's warning, but damned if that warning wouldn't come in handy.

When he reached her thighs he swallowed tightly as the fought the instinctive need to caress her. He could still smell her heat. It was soft and sweet, yearning. Son of a bitch, she was making his head spin, it was so intoxicating.

"Ease up," he murmured as she lifted her hips.

He jerked the material over the soft curves of her ass, his fingers itching to stroke them. The palms of his hands were nearly sweating with the hunger to caress her.

"All done." He tightened the drawstring marginally, making certain it wasn't snug against her sore midriff.

He knelt on the floor again and rolled the cuffs carefully over her bandaged feet. He wanted to resent her. Wanted to resent the necessity of taking care of her. Yet he couldn't. He had caught himself in the kitchen thinking of ways to ease her, to make things easier on her. Then he would remember he was supposed to be angry. Only to remember the horror stories he had heard in relationship to the experiments conducted on her. She was going to drive him crazy.

He was driving himself crazy trying to decide what he was supposed to feel, how he was supposed to act. This mating business was a pain in the ass, and now he knew well why he had wanted nothing to do with it. He had other things to do, other concerns that he felt was far more important than attempting to analyze these unfamiliar emotions.

"There you go. All done." He rose to his feet before bending down to lift her into his arms.

She was too light, almost fragile in his arms. She was also tense as hell and too damned weak to do more than just tighten against him as he carried her into the kitchen.

Once there, he set a bowl of stew before her and a tall glass of crisp, cold milk. She needed energy, food. Something that would stick with her and give her strength for the coming battles ahead.

"I have to go out for a while," he told her as he watched the delicate manner in which she ate.

She nodded sharply.

His lips twitched. She wasn't gobbling her food, but he'd be damned if he couldn't tell she wanted to. She kept careful control of herself, though, eating with a steady determination that hinted at the hunger she suffered from.

"Get as much rest as you can, Charity," he told her long minutes later as she sat back in her chair, replete, and glanced at him. "I'll be back to check on you sometime today. If you need me, there's a landline in the bedroom. It connects to the communications building. Just tell whoever answers that you need to speak to me."

"I'm sure I'll do fine without you." He didn't like the forced unconcern that suddenly surrounded her.

"I'm sure you will." At least he was certain she would try to make sure she needed him for nothing. "You need to rest for a few days, Charity. Get your strength back. I'll stay away as much as I can, but you know as well as I do that it's only to delay the inevitable."

She glanced at him from the corner of her eye.

"I need a bath." She didn't answer his comment. "Could you get someone to help me with that?"

His body tightened. He could see her, stretched out in the big tub in the bathroom, dressed in nothing but steam and heated water. His cock jerked in reflex.

Hell. Of course she needed a bath, he thought in weary disgust. The question was, could he maintain control long enough to help her with that?

"I'll help you." He tried to shrug as though he could do it with no problem, but already his body was heating further at the thought of it.

She watched him broodingly. He could see the battle going on in her head. She wanted the bath, desperately. She didn't want him helping her with it though.

Finally she sighed in resignation. "Fine. As long as I can get clean. The most I should need is help getting out of the tub. I can handle the rest of it on my own."

She should have been a Feline, he thought. Damned independent, stubborn female.

"Where am I anyway?" She suddenly grimaced as she stared around the kitchen. "Are we still in South America?"

"Colorado." He rose to his feet and cleared the table quickly. "The government allocated us several hundred acres here as a home base. The compound is heavily fortified with several dozen army personnel as well as Air Force support from the base across the mountain."

"The compound." She nodded then. "I'd heard of it. When I get better, I'd like to see it." She didn't look at him, and for all her appearance of unconcern he could tell it mattered to her to see what they had accomplished. Aiden didn't care much for the fact that it pleased him.

"When you can walk comfortably, I'll take you on a tour," he promised her softly as he moved to her drooping body.

"Come on. Let's get you back to bed. You need to nap a bit more before you're ready to do anything."

She sighed bleakly as he lifted her into his arms once more. "I don't sleep well, Aiden." She tried not to lean against his body. He could feel her tensing, holding herself away from him as she fought to maintain her control. He would allow it, for now, he thought.

"I have something that will help you sleep, baby." He laid her back on the bed before moving back to the kitchen.

When he returned, he carried a glass of water and a sedative Armani had approved for Hope and Faith last year.

"It's just a sedative," he told her when she stared at the small pill in his hand. "Our doctor had to create one especially for Hope and Faith. Sometimes, they don't sleep well either."

There was a single week of the month that the two women were more like rabid animals in their temperaments than grown women.

"Did she check…"

"She checked everything, Charity. Trust me, the damned woman doesn't miss a thing. Now take your medicine like a good girl so you can rest. You will need your strength soon." He gave her a wolfish smile. All teeth and male amusement.

Her eyes narrowed on him but she took the pill, swallowing it with a long drink of water before lying back against the pillows.

"Now sleep." He tucked the blankets around her. "I'll check on you later and help you get a bath."

Her eyes were closing even as he spoke. Aiden resisted the need to brush the hair back from her face, to caress the delicate line of her jaw. His fist clenched as he turned on his heel and stalked from the cabin before his need overcame his good sense. She was going to make him crazy, he thought. Then he grunted mockingly. Or perhaps she already had.

Chapter Eight

ဆ

The next morning, Charity was able to move more comfortably from the bed and to hobble through the house. Dressed in one of Aiden's T-shirts and another pair of drawstring sweat pants with the ankles rolled up quite a bit, she made her way through the small cabin in search of food.

She hadn't expected to awake alone. She had been prepared for yet another confrontation with Aiden, but the respite was more than appreciated. She was still weak, still tired. The months of experiments within the Labs had damned near killed her and she was smart enough to know that. It still could.

But at least she had slept for a change. She didn't know what was in the little pill Aiden had forced down her throat twice more the day before. But whatever it was it had thrown her into a sleep deep enough to allow her mind to ignore the pulsing arousal that tormented her. Unfortunately, it returned with a vengeance when she woke up.

Her body was sensitized, achy, the flesh tingling wherever she touched. Her cunt was moist, throbbing in longing. The sexual need that burned in her body seemed worse now, as though his touch had somehow stoked the fires already burning within her.

An hour later, the light meal finished, the dishes stacked in the sink, she looked around and admitted the silence of the cabin was starting to get to her. As much as she had prayed for peace over the past years, such silence was so foreign it was almost frightening to her.

From outside the cabin she could hear the sudden sounds of vehicles and voices raised as orders were shouted. It wasn't imperative, nor seemed alarming. Moving to the couch, she peaked outside the large window behind it to see what was going on.

The view was breathtaking. She ignored the movement going on in what appeared to be a central area of command in favor of the beauty of the mountains surrounding them. She needed to see more, ached to smell the breeze off the mountains. Standing up, she moved carefully to the front door.

The wounds on her feet hadn't been severe, thankfully, and she hoped within a few days they would be healed enough to allow her to more thoroughly investigate the Breed compound she had heard so much about in the past years.

The scientists she had worked with had been outraged, furious, when the United States had declared the Breeds were fully human. The explosion of outrage over the experiments and the uses the Council had envisioned for the Breeds had swept the world.

When the United States had apportioned the land in Colorado out to the Breeds and aided them in building the large protective compound, the fury within the Council had overflowed to the Labs. Recapturing or killing the Breeds was out of the question now. The focus of the world was frowning so heavily on those suspected and known of being within the Council, that any movement toward recouping their loses had been put on hold. Except for the Coyote Breeds. The Council had finally found the perfect soldier there. They followed orders precisely, their mercilessness nearly equal to their creators.

She stepped out on the porch, breathing in the clean, crisp air of the early fall morning and stared around with a sense of surprise.

A tall stone wall enclosed the acres-large compound. From where Aiden's cabin sat, slightly higher atop a rise, Charity could see the crystalline lake outside the enclosure, as well as the rolling hills that led to thickly forested mountains around them.

Inside the compound, friendly chaos seemed to reign. The cabins were set some distance apart, providing privacy and a sense of freedom, she thought. There were quite a few trees growing within the compound, a large blue pond, and several long, low buildings and storehouses. It was beginning to resemble a small town.

The central portion of the area was, at the moment, filled with dozens of men and women unloading boxes of equipment from several trucks that had pulled into the compound.

Guards watched from a safe distance, automatic rifles held in readiness as hard eyes watched the commotion. There had to be over a hundred Breeds milling about, as she could see. Which meant there were likely many others sleeping, working, doing whatever it took to keep the place running.

The entrance to the compound was heavily fortified and guarded as well. It would be damned near impossible to get in or out without being seen. And despite the beauty of the compound, it was still that…a heavily protected area.

Charity bit her lip as she eased herself onto the rough wood porch swing to the side of the porch, and continued to watch the work below. They were still imprisoned, just in a different way. The freedom she had always envisioned for the Breeds hadn't come about as she had thought it would.

As she watched the commotion going on, she realized her appearance on the porch hadn't gone unnoticed. She was being watched and carefully guarded. One of the men stood within a small stand of trees, the other in a fortified stand atop the compound wall. Both watched her with hard, determined gazes.

The enjoyment she had taken in feeling the breeze wash over her, smelling the clean, natural scent of the lake beyond and watching the men below at work suddenly dimmed. She rose to her feet and made her way carefully back into the house.

They didn't know, she thought. They couldn't know how she had helped them in the Labs, how she had helped plan their rescue. Few people did know. She had been a shadowy figure on the edge of the group working to destroy the Council and its mad schemes.

Not that they had succeeded. She pushed her fingers wearily through her hair as she stretched out on the couch and gazed moodily up at the ceiling. They were still creating, still experimenting, playing God and destroying lives.

The sudden opening of the door had her jerking upright, turning to watch as Aiden came into the cabin. He closed the door as he turned to look at her.

"Doing okay?" he asked her carefully.

"I was," she drawled. "Until a second ago."

Mocking amusement lit his eyes. "Too bad. I have to sleep sometime."

He bent over, unlacing his boots before toeing them off with a sigh of relief.

"You didn't sleep last night?" she asked him curiously, wondering what he had done.

"I was working last night." He moved to the kitchen.

"Working at what?" She frowned, realizing she had no idea what he did.

"Security." He shrugged. "I coordinate all the little details that keep the compound secure. We had someone sniffing around the perimeters of the wall last night."

"Coyotes?" she asked trying to still her fears. The Council would not let her go without trying to recapture her. The tests they had conducted on her were too important.

He shook his head. "I'm not certain. We could never tell for sure."

Charity watched silently as he pulled a bottle of water from the refrigerator and took a long drink. His head tilted back, revealing the stubborn curve of his chin, the strong line of his neck.

His dark flesh glistened with perspiration, the open collar of the cotton shirt revealed dark, tempting flesh. Her cunt clenched, her breasts aching as her gaze went to the hand wrapped around the bottle.

Large, strong hands, surprisingly graceful looking for a man.

"Have you eaten?" He lowered the bottle, placing it back in the refrigerator as he glanced at her.

"I ate." One hunger was satisfied, the other was killing her.

"I have to run into town in a bit," he told her. "Do a drive-through and see what I can see. Want to go with me?"

The invitation caught her off guard. She looked at him in surprise.

"What do you mean, see what you can see?" she asked him. "I thought you were going to go to sleep."

"Nap." He shrugged, watching her more closely now. "It's getting worse, Charity. Are you ready to stop fighting it yet?"

She shook her head. "What?" Confusion shot through her. She had no idea what his question meant.

"The arousal." He walked to her slowly, stopping at the edge of the couch, his eyes darkening. "We'd both sleep better if you stopped fighting it."

The amusement and knowledge in his voice and expression had her eyes narrowing in anger.

"Ah. I see." She folded her arms across her breasts. "So, everything would work out if I would just go ahead and let you fuck me. Right?"

He stilled then. Finally, after a long moment, he just shook his head as his expression flashed with regret.

He sighed wearily. "Forget it. I don't want to fight with you, Charity. This situation isn't sitting any easier with me. But facts are facts. You're in pain and I'm your best bet, baby, to escape it."

She'd rather die horny. The self-satisfied, egotistical bastard. What made it worse, was the knowledge that he was right.

"It gets easier." She shrugged. At least, it always had before. "How long was I unconscious anyway?" She frowned, wondering how much longer she had to wait.

She didn't like the grin that tilted his lips.

"Two days."

She thought quickly. "It should be over in a few more. I'll be fine."

He nodded. "Possibly. But what you're unaware of, sweet thing, was that I had to supply the blood transfusion you needed. That little anomaly in your blood system jumped by more than a hundred percent, according to the doctor. You're screwed, honey." Triumph glittered in his eyes, echoed in his voice.

Charity felt her heart jump in her breast. Her eyes widened in shock and fear. "No," she whispered, the implications of the information slapping her in the face. "No. You're lying."

"About what?" He frowned down at her. "I haven't lied to you about any part of it, Charity."

"The blood." She swallowed tightly. "Tell me, Aiden, you didn't give me blood."

His white teeth flashed as he smiled slowly. "Yeah, I did. Doc said it was the most amazing thing she ever saw. Your blood cells and those little Breed things I have in my blood were friggin' like crazy under that microscope. I think mine topped yours, honey. Doc is getting all kinds of ideas on how to help Faith and Hope now."

Weakness flooded her system. She pressed one hand to her abdomen, above the wound the scientists had made into her womb. She had no doubt in her mind the added component in his blood had dominated her blood cells. It made sense. The small amount contained in his semen had started the process; the addition of his unique blood was more than likely her downfall now.

She shook her head, fighting the tears threatening to flood her eyes.

"I need to talk to the doctor."

Aiden snorted. "You need to be fucked, sleep, then more sleep and food first. No way I'm letting you around that damned quack until you're stronger. The two of you are too damned much alike. You'll be strapped in an exam table first thing and the rest will be history. No."

"I have to see what you've done," she bit out, moving carefully to her feet, facing him, furious at him and the unknown doctor who had dared to transfuse her without tests first. "And why the hell did they give me your blood? Surely you had a supply of regular blood."

"We did." He nodded, crossing his arms over his broad chest. "Plenty of it. But none of it compatible to yours. We even had the right type, but tests showed a rejection of it from the anomaly in your blood. Only I matched, baby. Lucky you, huh?"

Sarcasm was thick, heavy in his voice.

"Do you have any idea what you've done?" She shook her head, almost dazed by the knowledge. "My body would have accepted my blood type. It may have protested mildly, but it would have accepted. You don't know what you've done."

"Oh, but I do," he informed her softly. "The transfusion merely cemented what we both know is true..."

She shook her head violently, limping away from him as her fingers clenched, fury washing over her.

"The drugs started this…"

"Nope." His voice was mild, if you discounted the dark savage throb beneath it. "When you went to your knees and swallowed my seed is what started it, Charity. You know it, and I know it. You were my weakness because nature decided that was the way it was. Not the drugs, not the blood."

She was trembling. Almost absently Charity was amazed at the tremors washing over her body. She stumbled against the fireplace, her breath hitching when he caught her, jerking her against his harder, hotter body.

"Feel it, Charity," he whispered in her ear. "It was there when I felt your mouth on my cock. It was there when I shot my come down your throat. It was there when you needed blood and I provided. You refused to let me escape, baby, now you can share the life I've built instead. Now doesn't that sound like fun?"

He was furious. Charity heard his anger, dark, deep, pulsing in his voice. He swung her up in his arms, ignoring her protesting cry as he stalked to the bedroom. His muscles were tight, tense and she could feel the need for violence that wrapped around him like an invisible flame.

But he was gentle as he laid her on the bed then sat beside her, staring down at her.

"I needed to save you," she whispered bleakly. "I had to."

"Because nature commanded," he bit out. "Whether you like it or not, Charity. Whether I wanted to accept it or not, you are my mate. Your blood proves it, but even more, this does…"

Before she could stop him his hand pushed beneath the loose pants and curved around her sensitive pussy, then his two long fingers plunged inside her soaked cunt as his palm pressed against the swollen clit.

"Aiden," she screamed out his name as her vagina convulsed, spilling more of her silky juices around his hard fingers.

"God, you're hot," he growled, his expression instantly filling with a hard, savage lust.

Her thighs clamped on his hand, her hands wrapping around his broad forearm, though she had little strength, little desire to pull him free. In fact, her body was so helpless, so desperately aroused she could do nothing but arch into the hand, silently begging for a deeper penetration.

He gave it to her. Slowly, his fingers stretched her, his gaze locking with hers as the rest of her vision seemed to darken.

"Aiden," she panted, terrified of her response to him, fighting herself and the needs washing over her.

"I bet you taste as good as you feel," he whispered. "And you feel damned good, baby. Too damned good. And you're too fucking weak for what I need right now."

He slid back slowly, ignoring her whimper, the arch of her hips.

"Aiden." She licked her lips, fighting the plea her body was screaming out to her.

He was breathing hard. Almost as hard as she was as he watched her closely, his eyes darkening with whatever thoughts were running through his mind.

"Rest," he growled. "Fucking rest, Charity, before I take you and hurt you worse than you already are."

Chapter Nine

ဢ

Aiden slammed out of the cabin, the need for sleep so overwhelmed by the need to fuck that he had to get away from her. He snorted, if only the need to fuck was what drove him, he thought as he plopped down on the steps and laced his boots on his feet.

He pushed his fingers restlessly through his hair as he tried to make sense of the impulses flowing through his brain. Damn, she was going to make him crazy. Just as crazy as he had been in the Labs after her arrival. Her scent had nearly taken him to his knees the first time she had walked into the room. The subtle, irresistible draw of her body had been almost more than he could bear.

He stared at the ground, sighing roughly. After the night spent roaming the mountains around the compound trying to track whoever or whatever had been outside the wall, he was exhausted. And it wasn't helping that his temper seemed so blasted iffy either. He was completely unsettled and he didn't care much for the feeling.

The woman was bewitching him. What the hell was wrong with him? She looked at him with those big hurt eyes, so filled with arousal and a deceptive warmth, and something inside him wanted to melt. It was inconvenient was what it was.

He lifted his head and stared off into the distance, wondering at the changes that were occurring too quickly around him. The changes within himself. He couldn't seem to make sense of it, and he'd be damned if he would go to Jacob and ask him anything about it. The other man watched him with such amusement now that it made his hackles rise instantly. But overriding it all was his need for Charity. The complete, compelling, unquenched need to fuck her as hard and as fast as he could drive his cock into her.

He gritted his teeth, standing almost painfully to his feet. That fickle flesh throbbed beneath the fly of his jeans with a demand that was damned near impossible to deny. As he started to stalk from the porch steps, the door to the cabin was flung open.

He turned, facing Charity warily as she stood there dressed in nothing but one of his T-shirts. And her nipples were hard. And he could smell her heat. And by God, she was his mate. He had waited six fucking years to touch her, to slake the need that never seemed to leave his body, and he was tired of waiting.

She opened her mouth to speak, then her eyes widened slowly as his narrowed. He stepped back to the rough plank porch, advancing on her as she watched him carefully. Her lips opened as she drew in a rough breath. Her breasts rose and fell quickly against the material of her borrowed shirt and the smell of her heat wrapped around him, tightening his cock, tensing his body with the unadulterated need to fuck.

"Go inside," he growled. "Leave the door closed. Don't step outside. Don't push me, don't berate me, Charity. I am one inch from pushing you against the damned wall and fucking you until we both collapse in exhaustion. I don't think you want that right now."

Her face flushed, her eyes darkening with arousal and fear. More arousal, though, than fear. Damn, she was killing him. A second ticked by, then another as her eyes slowly narrowed on him and anger replaced the fear.

"Aiden," she drawled mockingly as she leaned against the doorframe. "Is it a burden being such a prick or does it just come easy for you?"

He breathed in carefully, forcibly restraining himself to keep from touching her. From jerking her into his arms and pushing himself inside her tight, hot pussy he knew was waiting for him.

"Actually," he snarled. "It comes real fucking easy."

She sighed regretfully as she shook her head slowly. "I was afraid of that. Oh well…"

He moved in on her before she could finish, backing her into the house, then against the wall of the foyer. She stared up at him in surprise, fighting the arousal that sang through her blood as his dominance reflected in the savage features of his face. The Native American cast to his features had always enthralled her, now more so than ever.

"Charity," his voice was a hard, rumbling growl. "You can only push me so far. You can only deny me so long. Combine the two, and your time will shorten immeasurably. Do you understand me?"

She looked up at him through her lashes, her lips quirking teasingly, mockingly. "Beg me, baby, and we'll see." She threw his words back at him.

His fists clenched. If he touched her, he knew he would never release her. It wouldn't matter if she cried. It wouldn't matter if he hurt her. Some instinctive, primal need howled out its demand, making his body tremble as he fought to deny it. Just a while longer. Just until she was healed. Just until he knew he wouldn't physically hurt her.

"You are playing a very dangerous game," he breathed in roughly as he jerked back from her. "Be careful, Charity, that it doesn't backfire on you."

He stomped to the door once again.

"Will you be back for dinner, darlin'?" she asked him mockingly, stopping him in his tracks. His chest seemed clenched, something inside him screaming out for a tender voice, gentle words. He was a fool and he knew it.

He looked back at her, smiling slowly, confidently, his eyes going first to her hard-tipped breasts then to her seductive gaze. He watched her smile dim as her gaze dropped to the near lethal canines.

"I guess, mate," he growled. "It's all according to what you can come up with for dessert."

He gave her no time to respond but stalked as far and as fast from her as he could. He could feel the perspiration breaking out on his body as he fought for control. Fought the wild need to fuck, to mate, to have her beneath him screaming in climax as he thrust repeatedly inside her. It was a fight he was rapidly losing.

Chapter Ten

ഔ

The next afternoon, Charity hobbled through the connecting living room to the kitchen in search of food. She had slept away most of the day before, and long into the night, only awakening as Aiden checked on her after he returned. The arousal pulsing through her body was ever present, tormenting her dreams as deeply as it did her waking hours.

She was his mate. She knew that herself from the tests she had taken months after the episode in the Labs. Her body had begun changing then. The uncomfortable, ever present arousal. The surges of heat and irritation that seemed to linger just under her skin. Later, blood and saliva tests showed the presence of an unknown hormone that varied in strength according to the state of arousal she was in. She had hoped it would go away. Had hoped it would slowly diminish.

She hadn't counted on the scientists learning her secret, or finding a way to advance the changes her body was trying to make. She hadn't anticipated a damned blood transfusion, something even the scientists hadn't been able to use. The hormonal virus running through his blood was too potent for her body to fight.

But her heart and her mind disagreed. Nature was precise; it didn't make mistakes, not with something so basic as a mating instinct. Nature didn't deal with the heart, or anything as fickle as emotions. It dealt with biology, chemical reactions. A chemical reaction wasn't enough for her. Her heart, her soul, demanded more.

Charity eased her way to the stove and the pot sitting on the back burner as she made her way to the kitchen. Lifting the lid, she inhaled the scent of vegetables and beef, and a rich broth that made her mouth water.

Within minutes she was sitting down to the warm soup, and a cold glass of milk. As far as meals went, she figured it was as close to ambrosia as she was going to get. She couldn't remembering anything tasting as good in years. The milk was bitingly cold and eased the terrible dryness in her throat, while the food eased at least part of the cramps in her stomach.

She had just finished the small meal and placed her dishes in the sink to wash when a light knock sounded on the door and it opened slowly.

"Charity?" A female voice called out, and Charity watched in surprised as two women walked into the front room.

"Hope. Faith." Amazement filled her. They were older, filled out and more mature, but smiling in welcome as they rushed into the kitchen.

"Charity. Oh God, I thought you were dead or something." Faith reached her first.

Laughing, almost crying, Charity allowed the other woman to embrace her tightly, ignoring the sharp, burning protest from her flesh. Faith was a bit taller, her once long, auburn hair was cut shorter now, but there was no mistaking the pretty features or her laughter filled voice. Even in the Labs, after Faith got past her initial wariness, she had been filled with humor and a love of life.

As Faith moved back, Charity watched Hope quietly. Hope had hated all the scientists and Lab personnel after Wolfe's escape. The few times Charity had tried to contact her she had been rudely rebuffed.

"Thank you," Hope said quietly. "For Wolfe's life and his escape."

Surprise shot through her. "How did you know it was me?"

Hope's lips quirked into a grin. Her features were vaguely Asian, compliments of her Chinese mother. She had taken her slender height and blue eyes from her American father, though.

"I made it a point to find out, after Wolfe found me." She stepped closer, hugging Charity briefly, though warmly. "Come on now, get off those sore feet and we'll talk."

She hobbled back to the open living room, collapsing gratefully on the wide, well-cushioned couch as Hope disappeared into another room that Charity hadn't noticed earlier.

"Let's check your feet." She came back moments later carrying a first aid kit. "Dr. Armani will be around later this evening, but I'm sure they're starting to get uncomfortable again."

Armani. Charity controlled her expression, her knowledge of the doctor. Armani had been her contact while she was with the Council, until more than a year ago. Surely to God Armani had known better than to transfuse her with Aiden's blood.

"They're actually not too bad." Charity shrugged, uncomfortable with having the other woman kneeling at her feet. "I could use some clothes, though."

"I have some stuff you can wear. I'll run over to the cabin and get them while Hope takes care of this." No sooner than she spoke the other woman turned and rushed back out the front door.

"She's still in heat," Hope sighed, shaking her head. "Can't sit still for a minute."

"As are you." Charity caught the slight, though distinct scent of a storm around the other woman as well. "How long have you and Wolfe been back together?"

Hope glanced up at her, her dark blue eyes somber. "Almost a year. And yes, I am. It eases somewhat, sometimes. But it's still pretty strong. It's eased for me, for the time being."

"Have your hormonal levels been tested while it's strongest?" Charity asked her, wincing as Hope checked the tender pads of her feet. "My own tests showed increased hormone levels during ovulation. The scientists later found a slight genetic alteration in the cell structure of the ovaries. Their tests began there. With each successive hormonal treatment I was given, the cell structure has changed further, coming closer to a match with the Wolf Breed sperm. Have you been tested for any of these changes?"

The unique DNA coding of the male Breed ruled out breeding with either Breed, or non-Breed females. Yet the scientists were finding a way to break through this barrier.

"No." Hope shook her head slowly. "Wolfe banned any such testing, and honestly, we didn't see the need."

"Hope, that can't continue." Charity frowned fiercely. "Listen to me, your body is changing. Slowly. Evolving to match Wolfe's enough to breed. This has to be watched carefully. It affects any woman that would mate with a Breed male. The answer to this is in the blood. The anomaly in the Breed blood cells is like a virus to the right woman, if the chemistry is compatible. It then infects the ovaries and the egg, making conception possible with the compatible sperm."

"Why would the scientists try to advance this? Or nature?" Shock filled Hope's expression as she stared up at him in concern. "The original object was to prevent breeding."

Charity took a deep breath, trying to tamp back her own fears. "They want the children, Hope, to experiment on. Animals whose organs will come closer to matching human requirements. Disposable creations for experimentation. They haven't stopped. They will never stop. And no one, not Breed, nor mate nor child will ever be safe from them. Their super Army didn't come to fruition, so they've changed direction now. A direction that could become more dangerous than their original plans. As for nature..." She took a deep, trembling breath. "I don't know why, but I know the evolution began in me, after I the night I swallowed Aiden's semen. It's similar to a virus at the cellular level. It's so complicated even the Council scientists have been unable to figure it out completely. But it begins a slow evolution that I believe will result in conception. As though nature itself has decided that the species will survive."

She watched as Hope's face paled. "Did you tell Aiden this?" she whispered desperately. "Does he know?"

Charity shook her head. "Keegan knew. I assumed he had found time to talk to Wolfe."

Hope shook her head imperatively. "Keegan hasn't said anything, Charity. Nothing. The Winged Breeds disappeared within hours of their rescue. No one has seen them."

No one? Keegan held the answers, the key to all this. He had told her, right before the attack on the mountain, that he had figured it out. That he knew what the scientists were doing, and how nature would eventually fight back. He had kept her sane those last days as he connected with her, explaining what her body was doing, and why. He wouldn't just leave.

"No." Charity blinked at her in surprise. "Keegan wouldn't do that. He knows the experiments. He knows what they were doing, step by step, even when I didn't. Hope, Keegan is incredibly psychic, with a photographic memory. He was connected to me during those experiments. He knows everything, every last detail, he wouldn't just leave."

Hope stood to her feet, the first aid kit and Charity's raw feet forgotten as she panted for breath. "I have to find Wolfe. This is worse than any of us believed."

She rushed from the house, the door slamming behind her as Charity covered her face with her hands before pushing her fingers through her hair with weary frustration.

"Where are you, Keegan?" she bit out furiously, rubbing her temples, fighting for the connection he had often kept with her. Unable to believe he would just disappear, just leave. "Damn you, why the hell did you run?"

The mental connection she had once shared with him was absent, though. She felt only silence, only a bleak desertion by the man she had thought was a friend.

It made no sense. Keegan wasn't the type to just drop a responsibility he had taken on. He knew he would be needed. Knew Charity would need the information he had gathered as he shared those experiments with her telepathically. It was the reason she had allowed him to set up the link in the first place.

Frowning, she fought to re-establish the connection then sighed in bleak resignation. Keegan had always come to her. She had never had to call out to him, to try to find him; he had just been there. A presence she had been able to feel whenever she needed to maintain control, or when the pain became too blinding to focus for herself.

And now he was just gone. Her eyes narrowed. What was he up to? She knew he was calculating, secretive. He wouldn't have left in such a way unless there had been a reason for it. Unless the danger was increased somehow by his presence. She bit her lip thoughtfully. He was up to something. She could feel it. She knew him well enough to know how he plotted, planned. Now, she just had to figure out what he was up to, and why.

Chapter Eleven

ഌ

Aiden stood quietly behind the chair Wolfe sat in, while Jacob stood more to his side. His pistol was strapped to his thigh, along the wall behind him a rack of automatic weapons were held, ready for use. As the leader of the controversial Wolf Breed Packs, protecting his life could sometimes become a job in itself. At the moment, the room held not just Wolfe and his mate, but Jacob and his as well. Other than Charity, these two women were the only known mated females. That they were also the mates to the head of the Packs made them even more important.

The news that Hope had brought to Wolfe earlier was already beginning to cause a stir in the small Breed compound. Gathered in the room were the Leaders of the four packs who had pledged their loyalty to Wolfe and to the newly formed Breed Alliance. They all listened with bated breath as Hope explained Charity's information. Information she had not given him, but had given to another instead. Information he would have much preferred that she keep to herself for a bit longer.

"To verify this, I'd have to run my own tests." Dr. Armani was thoughtful as she watched Wolfe. "There's no way I will consider accepting this information on hear-say alone." She glanced at Hope apologetically. "Charity's blood tests alone tell me it's possible, but I refuse to go in blind."

"Charity is already pumped full of the drugs, she would be perfect…" Hope began.

"No." Aiden's head rose in shock and anger as Hope voiced the thought. He speared her with a dark glance, his jaw clenching tightly as he fought to control the instinctive anger.

More experiments? The pain he had watched ravage Charity's body, even while unconscious, had nearly destroyed him. He wouldn't consider such an action.

"Aiden, hear her out," Wolfe said quietly.

Aiden growled, for the first time that he could remember, so opposed to his leader that he feared his own reactions.

"I refuse to allow it," he bit out, pacing around the couch, aware of the other members of the Council watching him carefully. "She is not part of this Pack, Wolfe, and therefore not under your command. She is mine…"

"And you are under my command." Wolfe glanced at him, his gaze reflective.

Aiden narrowed his eyes, watching the other man intently. He had never known Wolfe to issue an order he didn't agree with. Never known the other man to ask of others what he would not do himself. But this, Aiden would not consider.

"She is my mate," he snarled, his body hardening, tightening at the thought of her unclaimed status. "It is not for you to order me there, Wolfe."

Wolfe sighed. "Unfortunately you are right, Aiden. But it is not for you to choose for her. Charity will be given the choice."

"No…"

"Aiden. Our very survival depends on our ability to breed. Hope and Faith are in constant arousal now, their bodies no longer their own, their sexuality no longer theirs to control. If there is a way to stop this, then it is not something we can overlook," Wolfe snapped in frustration.

Aiden well understood his leader's anger and concern. He glanced at his sister in frustration, seeing her compassion, her understanding as she watched him. But he also saw well the signs of her growing arousal once again. Both women were unable to be away from their mates for very long. The situation was breeding nothing but anger and more frustration.

"The blood work I've run up to this point supports Charity's claims," Dr. Armani said softly in the silence of the room. "The tests I would require would be done gently, Aiden, with all care given to your mate's body and her mind. I don't wish to harm her. But we must see the results of the drugs they used on her. It could help me, perhaps, to determine how to recreate the process in a gentler manner."

"It seems to me it would be smarter to find those damned Winged bastards," Aiden snarled. "They have the answers."

"Doesn't matter. Charity's body holds the key. We could do nothing without examining her to see the results of whatever information Keegan holds," the doctor snapped out. "Stop being so damned possessive, Aiden. I'm not going to hurt her."

His head swung around as he fought a furious growl. The doctor was watching him as she would a recalcitrant child. The look didn't set well with him.

"You are right. You will not hurt her, because there will be no tests," he bit out.

"Aren't you the same man who claimed this woman was not his mate? Nothing to him?" the doctor asked as she crossed her arms under her breasts, watching him mockingly. "What do you care what is done with her body? She is not a Breed, Aiden, and nothing to you."

"Do not play word games with me, Armani," he snapped, infuriated that she would throw his own angry words back at him. "She has yet to heal from whatever hell they put her through. This has nothing to do with a mating and everything to do with a healing. I will not allow it."

"A healing will not occur, Aiden, until possibly, conception," the doctor snapped back, her black eyes glittering with her own ire. "Do not presume to believe that, whatever those experiments were, the effects will merely wash away now that she is safe. You know better than this."

Aiden felt his stomach tighten with a sensation akin to fear. Conception? He clenched his fists as he fought to hold back the blistering curses raging through his mind. Dammit, Charity wasn't strong enough to hold herself up right now, let alone to survive the unknown trials of a Breed birth. Only God knew what would result.

"Aiden." Wolfe came to his feet, his expression stoic, his gaze compassionate. "This is not any easier on our women, Hope and Faith, as well as those who will suffer through this when they mate. If Charity holds the answers, then we must find out what they are."

"Personally, I think you're talking to the wrong person about this," Hope spoke up then, her gaze leveled on Aiden. "Charity has conducted her own experiments, and she knows this won't merely go away. I say we ask her."

"I say she's too weak," Aiden shook his head roughly. "Not now. Not until she has strengthened."

"Aiden, I just saw your woman not more than an hour ago," Hope argued. "She is in such need her body trembles from it. I've never seen Faith, nor known myself, to suffer so excessively from the heat. It's her pain, therefore it's her choice."

"It will be a child as well, Hope, should she conceive," he growled. "Have you forgotten so easily how familiar she was with your mother? How easily she betrayed me?"

"You mean how easily she saved your worthless hide." Faith stepped into the fray then. "I remember how nobly you were willing to give up your life on a whim, brother, and how she saved it. I do not see that as a betrayal."

"Aiden." Wolfe forestalled anything he would have said to his sister in the heat of anger. "Remember, Charity is not the only one who will feel the effects of this arousal. Return to your mate, discuss this if you will, or take care of the needs tormenting you both first, whichever you deem more important. But unless Keegan is found in the next few days, then this discussion will be resolved. To all our satisfaction."

Aiden drew in a hard, controlling breath. Wolfe watched him without a hint of leniency in his expression. He would not change his mind if no other answer were found.

"Would you so willingly give over your woman, Wolfe?" he snarled viciously.

Wolfe sighed wearily as he glanced at the woman in question. "To ease her torment, Aiden, I would do whatever is necessary," he finally sighed softly. "If it meant my own life, I would give it to ease Hope's way." He turned back to him slowly. "But that is my love for her. My understanding of her pain. From where, Aiden, does your reluctance stem?"

Aiden raised his head slowly, proudly. "From ownership, Wolfe. The bitch is mine. Not yours, not the Pack's. Mine. Remember that before you come to my cabin claiming her in the name of your love for your mate."

He turned and stalked from the lead cabin, his boots thumping loudly, the door slamming with a satisfying thump behind him. The cool night air wrapped around him, embracing him with a sense of freedom, of wonder. And yet his soul felt as helplessly bound as it had been for six long, torturous years.

* * * * *

"What do you think?" Wolfe turned to Jacob, who had stayed silent, watchful as the confrontation arose with Aiden.

Wolfe felt torn, placed between his friend and the needs of Hope and Faith, as well as Charity. The scent of her need was nearly overpowering the last time he had been in Aiden's cabin. Even unconscious her body had sought relief, in whatever form it could find.

He watched Jacob frown consideringly before his lips twisted in a wry grin. "He's a goner." He shrugged. "Give him long enough to sate himself the first time with her, and he'll think more clearly then."

"If she's strong enough to handle it." Wolfe shook his head wearily then turned to the doctor for her opinion. The more unusual aspects of Breed mating had the potential to terrify, more than to arouse, unsuspecting females.

Dr. Armani arched a brow in mocking question. "You're asking me? Sorry, Wolfe, I have yet to understand the regular mating process you go through. The anal aspects are even more confusing."

"It eases the arousal, for a time," Hope reminded her. "So it must have significance."

"Of course. I'm certain it does." She tucked her hands into the pockets of her light jacket. "That doesn't mean I know what it is yet. And if Aiden has his way, it appears I never will."

Wolfe growled. "Find that fucking Winged Breed." He turned on Jacob again. "Send out one of our best groups. They have to be in that damned jungle somewhere. If you have to, put out a call to Sam's group. I want them found."

"Two Packs are already there, Wolfe." Jacob shook his head, grimacing. "If they can find them then they will. I'll call in Sam, but I don't like the idea of it. Either way, I have a feeling Keegan or his people won't show themselves until they have no other choice. Unfortunately, I have no idea what would push them to it."

Wolfe drew in a deep breath, tamping down his own anger, his own frustration. His own arousal. Aiden's woman wasn't the only one in heat, and Aiden's patience wasn't the only one being pushed to its limits. If they didn't find an answer to this soon, then there would be no hope for any of them, let alone their futures.

Chapter Twelve

&

She was breathing through the contractions ripping her womb apart. Aiden watched from the doorway, his mind consumed with such contradictory impulses that he wasn't certain if he should leave, or if he should go to her. His body demanded he go to her. Every bone and muscle in his body, not to mention his traitorous cock, demanded that he take her now.

His control, so fiercely won after she had taken it from him, demanded that he run. Run hard and fast, as far away from this woman as he could get. The emotional threat she represented tore at him. The mating to come terrified him. Already he could feel the aggression, the dominance roaring within his body.

Wolfe and Aiden had warned him of what was to come, but had anyone warned her? No one had, he knew. Hope and Faith hadn't been with her long enough, and he knew her earlier fear of their mating would only magnify if he explained the full details of it to her. Anal sex would frighten any virgin in such circumstances. To be taken in such a manner by a Breed male would be terrifying at first.

He pushed his fingers through his hair, fighting himself, fighting the urges running through him. How was he supposed to steel his heart against her? She had known rescue was coming, had fought to save him when he would have willingly died to escape the hell he knew was coming.

Had it really been her fault...his loss of control?

She moaned weakly, curling tighter into the fetal position she had assumed, holding a pillow tight to her stomach. Cian had told them that her pain had only grown worse over the months. Each injection had pushed her closer to insanity as she fought the changes ripping through her body. Changes that were slowly preparing her for him.

His hands went to his shirt, releasing the buttons slowly as he fought to maintain control of his breathing. Her scent was rich and evocative, filled with the power of a mountain storm, the heady fragrance of honeysuckle. His cock was like a staff of burning iron, throbbing beneath the restriction of his jeans, pleading for the tight confines of her honey-rich cunt. She would be wet, slick and hot. Her channel would clasp him like a wet velvet fist, dragging over his sensitive flesh as he thrust in and out. He swallowed tightly at the thought.

It only took moments for him to undress. He left his clothes where they fell then padded slowly to the bed. She was his mate. God help them both, but he couldn't leave her in pain, nor could he bear his own any longer.

"Charity," he whispered as he moved onto the bed behind her, reaching out to draw her hair back from her perspiring face.

"Go away, Aiden." Her voice was strangled, thick. "I can't think while you're here."

He frowned down at her. "You aren't thinking, Charity, you are in too much pain to think."

"The contractions are worse," she gritted out. "The heat is worse, when it should be leveling off. There's a difference to it now. It has to be because of the transfusion. I need a fucking lab." She was almost crying now. "How am I supposed to figure this out without tests? Without equipment? Goddammit, get away from me." She was panting for air now.

Aiden shook his head in confusion. She seemed more concerned with testing her damned reactions than she was with alleviating the pain. He lay down beside her, his arm hooking over her waist and pulling her back against his body.

She gasped, her body stiffening before a moan escaped her throat.

"God, you're so warm," she whispered, burying her head in the pillow beneath her. "How am I supposed to fight this when you're so damned warm, Aiden?"

He closed his eyes. He couldn't halt the need to kiss the soft shell of her ear. Her breath caught as a shiver trembled over her body.

"I'm scared, Aiden," she whispered, her voice sounding lost, lonely. "I don't know how to fight this when you're so close to me. And I don't think I can bear your hatred when it's over."

He breathed out roughly. "If only I could hate you, Charity." His hand moved beneath the pillow she had gripped to her stomach.

The contractions were harder than they had been before. He moved his hand beneath her shirt, beginning a gentle massaging motion with his fingers as her breathing began to deepen, roughen.

"Feel good?" he asked, noticing her reaction as his breath whispered over her ear.

"Too good," she moaned. "I can't think, Aiden."

"Do not think at all, Charity." He closed his eyes, drawing in her scent, becoming nearly intoxicated on the sweetness of it.

His body was clamoring now. He clenched his teeth as his lips smoothed over her neck. Her blood beat hard and fast beneath the tender skin as her body tightened further.

She swallowed tightly. "What you said earlier..." He could hear the fear in her voice.

"Neither Hope nor Faith have known any pain from the dominance of their mates, or the matings themselves, Charity. Your body is ready for me, and what is not yet prepared, will be prepared in due time."

His cock was pressed against the crease of her buttocks. Below, the small tight hole of her anus awaited him. He hadn't believed Wolfe and Aiden when they warned him of that overwhelming desire to possess that dark, forbidden spot. But he believed them now. His throttled growl shocked them both as he fought to deny himself. She was already frightened, he knew. To take her there, to force himself into the narrow depths of her anus, could very well terrify her. Yet, the need was like a fever flowing hard and fast through his veins.

Prepare her. He had to prepare her. If her arousal were high enough, her needs overwhelming even her fears, then she would be ready for him.

"Come here to me, Charity." He pulled the pillow from her grasp then rolled her over to her back.

She stared up at him, her brown eyes dark, dazed with her arousal as he stared down at her.

"See how your body eases for me," he said gently, his hand pressed to her stomach, easing the knots from the muscles of her abdomen. "It knows I can relieve the pain, the arousal. Only my body can do this for you, Charity. Only my touch."

He pushed the T-shirt up her body, remembering heatedly how he had torn the other one from her. He undressed her quickly, tossing the fabric from the bed as he stared down at the beauty displayed before him.

Her breasts rose and fell in a hard, fast rhythm. Perspiration glistened on the silken skin, emphasizing the swollen curves and dark, elongated nipples. He tore his gaze from the ripe mounds, meeting hers as he fought for control.

"I'll conceive," she reminded him again, tears glistening in her eyes. "I don't want a child, Aiden. I don't want to bring another into such a hopeless situation."

His lips quirked at her accurate description of the Breeds' lives to this point. It was often a hopeless battle they fought.

"Nature will do what it must." He pulled her slowly into his arms then. "Our concern, Charity, is to aid it as best we can. No matter the cost. We survive, because we must."

He gave her no chance to answer or to argue. His head lowered. The temptation of her lips, swollen from the sensuality of her arousal, was too much to resist. Like the sweetest fruit, demanding that he taste of its erotic perfection.

She whimpered when his lips touched hers, opening to him, her hands moving timidly to his shoulders as his fingers continued to stroke her tightened abdomen.

She was as intoxicating, as he knew she would be. Aiden allowed his tongue to stroke over her trembling lips, ignoring her soft entreaty as they opened for the silken feel of the plump curves beneath his tongue. She was moving against him slowly, her nipples raking over his chest like little brands of need.

Control was a tenuous thing at best, but he found pride in the fact that he was holding onto his. Until she arched against him, a hungry moan breaking from her throat as her tongue reached out to lick back at him.

Chapter Thirteen

ဆ

The teasing, licking strokes at her lips were driving her crazy. Charity had hungered for Aiden's kiss, his touch, for too long. As the pain in her abdomen slowly began to ease, another torturous ache took its place. The fires in her cunt began to flame through her body, clouding her mind with an arousal too fierce to fight any longer.

As she stroked across his tongue, a growl, deep and rough, sounded in his chest a second before it plunged hard and hot inside the depths of her mouth. His arm pushed beneath her shoulders as the other went around her waist, jerking her closer, tighter to his chest as she tasted the wildness of his kiss. Spicy and addicting, the moist stroke of his tongue inflamed her further.

As hers tangled with it, she felt the small swollen glands at the side, though paid little attention to them. Yet another strange occurrence for this unusual Breed. He moved further over her, stroking the interior of her mouth, her lips, her tongue, the edge of her teeth until she clamped her lips on the teasing invader and suckled at it desperately.

The taste that filled her mouth sent her senses spinning. She wouldn't have believed lust could have its own unique flavor, but Aiden's did. It tasted of a summer thunderstorm, quenching her thirst for his passion but only driving her hunger for his touch higher. The taste filled her, intoxicated her, made her desperate for more. It made her as wild as his taste.

She twisted in his arms, pressing harder against him. She needed, ached for more. What the "more" was, she wasn't certain at that point. But her entire body felt inflamed, her arousal building higher, to heights she never dreamed of knowing.

Each time she drew on his tongue the taste of his lust filled her. Within seconds her body was burning brighter. As though the very essence of his kiss was an aphrodisiac all its own. It was worse than any of the drugs forced into her body. More blinding, more intense than anything else she had known in her life.

He growled into her mouth then, pulling back, his teeth nipping at her lips as she fought to draw him back to her. He controlled her struggles easily as his lips moved down her neck, his canines raking her skin as she shuddered at the pleasure of it.

"Aiden, don't torment me this way." Her cunt was on fire. She could feel the flames licking through the tissue there, traveling to her womb, stroking it with the lava-hot agony of her arousal.

"Soon." His voice was a rough, untamed growl. "First. First I will do as I have dreamed of for years."

He held her wrists to the bed as he paused over her heaving breasts. Charity watched him, barely able to keep her eyes opened, fighting for breath as she marveled at the sensuality shaping his face.

"Aiden..." She trembled beneath his brooding, hot gaze as it focused on her swollen curves.

"How pretty they are," he breathed out roughly. "How many years I've dreamed of tasting your sweet breasts, Charity. Feeling your nipples in my mouth, against my tongue. Hard and aching for my touch."

He licked his lips and Charity moaned against the punch of lust that contracted her womb. No pain this time, just a brutal contraction of agonized desire that halted her breath. Then his tongue distended and she whimpered. When it stroked against one overly sensitized nipple she arched violently to him, a cry of pleasure erupting from her throat.

When the heat of his mouth covered the hard tip, pleasure whipped through her body with such force that she jerked with it, an almost orgasmic sensation ripping through her.

"Aiden please." She pressed against him, gasping for breath as his lips suckled at her breast, his tongue stroking her nipple with diabolical intent as his hands held hers shackled, refusing to allow her to touch him in turn.

He moaned against her sensitive flesh, his canines rasping against her as he nipped at her nipple then. A small flash of fire, of never-ending intensity, seared across the heated peak.

Each touch made her body weaker, made her arousal flare higher. As though his touch alone was more potent than the drugs injected into her body. She stared down at him, fighting to breathe as his head began to lower, his lips stroking down the tightened muscles of her stomach.

Each caress was like a living flame on her skin. Each stroke of his tongue only fanned it higher, hotter, brighter.

"Charity," he whispered her name as he reached the clenching muscles of her abdomen. "The scent of your need is making me crazy."

Making him crazy? She was on the verge of melting into a puddle of lust, and he said she was making him crazy?

He released her hands as he moved lower, but there was no danger of her protesting now. She was panting, weakened by the surging pleasures, the blistering heat in her vagina.

His lips stroked over her, dipping into the small valley of her belly button, moving steadily closer to the swollen, moist curves of her bare cunt. Charity could only watch, could only tremble in anticipation as the room seemed to heat with the building sensuality stretching between them.

When his tongue stroked over her swollen clit, circling it with a smooth, sensuous lick she couldn't halt the moaning cry for relief, or the spasmodic jerk of her hips as she desperately sought a deeper touch.

"Aiden, this will kill me..." She broke up, a strangled scream erupting from her throat as his lips covered her, drawing her sensitive clit into his suckling mouth.

There was heat and fire, and then there was mindless ecstasy. It overtook her, wrapping her in the cataclysmic folds of an impending orgasm that she knew would destroy her forever.

His tongue licked and stroked, rasping over the sensitized knot of nerves as his hands held her thighs open, controlling her involuntary undulations against his mouth. Her vagina spilled its silky moisture, then rippled in agonized anticipation as his fingers parted the swollen flesh protecting its entrance.

"Charity," he growled against the throbbing knot of nerves as his fingers slid through the thick essence. "I cannot wait much longer."

"Don't wait," she gasped, her hips arching to the whisper of his ragged breaths as her clit screamed out at the desertion. "For God's sake, Aiden, please. Please make me come."

One long finger thrust hard and deep inside the tight channel as his mouth returned to her clit with hungry demand. His mouth covered her again, greedy, hungry in his greed. Charity's eyes widened, her gaze darkening as sensation began to erupt inside her.

Her clitoris fragmented into a fireworks explosion of ecstasy as her vagina tightened on the invading finger, pulsed then erupted in rapture. The whipping sensations tore through her, tightening her muscles as heat flamed throughout her body. She screamed his name, only barely aware of him moving as the lightning strokes of pleasure tore her apart.

In the midst of the incredible array of fiery explosions, Aiden moved over her and positioned himself quickly. He hesitated for only a moment, but long enough for Charity to feel the sudden, heated warmth that exploded from the head of his cock. She stared up at him in surprise, watching his eyes widen.

He nudged inside her further. The heated expulsion repeated, and incredibly she felt her vagina warming, relaxing, yet firing a deeper need inside the hungry depths.

"What..." She shook as the hunger became a compulsion, a hard demand that left her gasping.

"Charity, forgive me." He grimaced, then with one hard stroke filled the swollen, hungry depths of her cunt with his thick erection.

She climaxed once more on the first stroke. She couldn't breathe. She gasped for breath, her head whipping against the mattress as her hands flailed helplessly to hold onto the bulging breadth of his arm as he braced himself on his elbows.

His features looked distorted as she fought to focus on his face. She couldn't fight the sensations. Couldn't fight the building surge of renewed hunger. His cock filled her as it surged through swollen tissue, but the bite of pain did little to cool the violent arousal that pushed her past any previous perceptions of need.

"Aiden. Aiden, help me." She couldn't stop the tortured whisper as she felt his lips caress her shoulder, his teeth raking her. "Please...Aiden, please. Do something."

Despite the echoes of release that still rippled over her body, she needed more.

Aiden groaned at her shoulder, his arms holding her close as he began to move. The hot shaft of engorged flesh dragged past the gripping muscles of her cunt, only to return in a hard stroke of such brutal pleasure that she swore it would kill her. Pain bit at the outer edges of sensation, but even that only drove her higher.

"Mine," he growled then. "Do you hear me, Charity? Mine."

His cock thrust into her greedy, clenching cunt with almost mindless fervor. The smooth hard strokes kept her body clamoring for more as the sensations intensified, built; growing into such a conflagration she could only gasp at the power. And with each stroke, felt the hard, tortured knot of need tightening in her womb.

Her thighs tensed, the muscles of her cunt involuntarily tightening on the surging shaft, feeling the thick veins, the throb of blood, the hard pulse that beat beneath the engorged flesh, and she knew his control was slipping.

"More," he gasped, his hands lowering, gripping her thighs and forcing her legs to raise.

He lay over her, his mouth at her shoulder, his teeth an erotic pressure on her skin as he began to fuck her hard, deep. She could feel his cock battering at the entrance to her womb, stroking her higher, filling her, driving her farther into the brutal maelstrom of sensation.

When her orgasm came, Charity knew she had died. Her breath gurgled in her throat, her eyes blinded as her womb tightened further, then further. She tried to scream when she felt the implosion, but there was no breath for sound. She didn't explode outward, but inward. A violent internal destruction that occurred with such pleasure she knew she would never survive the ordeal.

She felt her own release splatter past his surging cock, then amazingly, her muscles clamped tighter on him, tighter...

"Aiden..." Reality ceased to exist as she simultaneously felt his teeth lock onto her shoulder as his cock began to swell.

She fought it. Fought him. The agonizing swell of pleasure, the feeling of a fist-sized knot growing halfway down the shaft was too much. Her body pulsed in frenzied orgasm as she tightened further, trying to force him away. She couldn't move. With his teeth locked into her shoulder, his animalistic growls sounding in her ear as his cock swelled, she couldn't force him away.

Another smaller orgasm ripped through her body then as she felt the first splash of his hot seed inside her quaking pussy. His cock was pulsing hard, the beat of blood vibrating through her over-stretched muscles as his cock jerked inside her, spilling the thick, rich semen that seemed to soak into every cell it touched.

His hips jerked, his cock straining to thrust inside her farther as they both cried out at the pleasure/pain of it.

"God, yes," he groaned, as his mouth lifted from her shoulder. "All of it, Charity. Take all of it."

The knot pulsed, engorged, pushing her into another series of rapid explosions as yet more of his release surged inside the sealed channel. There would be no loss of seed. She could nearly feel her womb sucking each drop of it inside its hungry depths.

The head of his cock was buried against her cervix, each time her own hips jerked, she could feel the bulging head moving against it. Each eruption from the thick crown shot straight inside the opening, drenching her womb.

Minutes, hours later, the painful sensitivity through the rest of her body eased, though Aiden stayed locked tight inside her. His weight was now held on his elbows, though his head dropped against her shoulder. His damp hair caressed her cheek as his heaving chest rasped against her tender nipples.

For the first time in six years, Charity felt her body ease. For the first time in six months, she felt the horrible pain disintegrate. She sighed, her arms falling to the bed as exhaustion began to overtake her.

"I'm sorry," she whispered, sighing deeply. "I need to sleep now, Aiden. I haven't slept in so long…"

She had been unconscious, but even then tormented with her body's needs. With the inner fires of desperation quenched, the need for true rest overtook her.

Aiden would protect her, just as he had eased her. That thought comforted her as she finally gave into the weariness. Her eyes closed as she breathed out deeply, then darkness overwhelmed her. Sleep, she thought. Finally, sleep.

Chapter Fourteen

ဢ

Aiden groaned roughly as he slid his sensitized flesh from the wet clasp of Charity's tight vagina. The slick, moist sound as he slid from her had his cock twitching with the need to bury inside her once again, though he knew that such an option was, for now, impossible.

He stared down at her, unable to make himself move entirely from her. Her short, dark blonde hair was damp, several strands clinging to the moist features of her face. Perspiration coated her body and ran in shallow rivulets to the sheets below her.

He touched her flushed cheek with the fingers of one hand, his thumb moving to caress the swollen contours of her lips. Asleep, she looked fragile, innocent, exhausted.

Lines of weariness creased her face. The complete submission of her body to the sleep that had overtaken her went deeper than the unconsciousness that had held her after her escape. This was bone-deep, and soul-weary. How long, he wondered, had she been without restful sleep?

He walked into the bathroom and collected a small wash pan, cloth, soap and towel and returned to the bed. He couldn't let her sleep with the sweat and semen drying on her sensitive skin. She wouldn't rest well, and suddenly, knowing that she slept well was of primary importance to him.

He sponged her off carefully, ignoring the hard throb of his cock while enjoying the satiny softness of her skin. From head to toe he cleaned her, ignoring her grumbling moans, his lips quirking in a smile as she finally rolled to her stomach to avoid him.

And there temptation reigned. He sponged her shoulders, the graceful line of her back, her slender legs and tempting thighs. He paused before carefully washing the soft contours of her buttocks then drying them slowly. His fingers trembled as he ran the dry towel down the shadowed cleft of her rear. His cock throbbed in hard demand.

He wasn't satisfied by a long shot. He needed her again, harder, deeper, until his cock could swell and explode inside her once more. Right there. His fingers glanced over the tight little entrance to her anus. He needed her there.

His disgusted curse was a silent expulsion of air as he moved from the bed. He returned the basin to the bathroom, then set about changing the sheets of the bed as smoothly as possible.

She grumbled irritably but continued to sleep as he finally tucked the fitted ends on both sides of the mattress. A clean sheet covered her then, as well as one of the quilts the women from a nearby town had donated.

She lay on her stomach, almost boneless, her breathing even and deep as she slept. The dark blonde strands of her hair fell silky and soft to her shoulders, though still damp from her earlier passion. He remembered how long it had once been, falling nearly to her hips in a fall of silk. Why had she cut it, he wondered. And why did he care?

He grimaced at the thought as he made himself leave the bedroom. She had once again turned his world upside down and he was left to deal with it as she slept.

Sometime between finding her once again, and finally taking her, he had accepted the mating. He had known in those damned Labs that his connection to her was unbreakable. She could make him respond when no one else could. She softened him when he wanted to be cruel; she had given him hope when he had thought it was futile.

Aiden stepped out onto the porch of the cabin, gazing out at the darkness of night, which had fallen over the compound.

He could barely glimpse the high walls that ringed the ten-acre compound. Set with motion sensors and guarded by a team of highly trained enforcers and guard dogs, the chances of the area being breached were slim. But they were still enclosed, imprisoned in many ways. There was no place on earth that was truly safe.

The compound now held over two hundred Wolf Breed inhabitants, from the ages of sixteen to early thirties, and more straggled in monthly. There were several small prides of Feline Breeds that had come in, but they were quickly transferred to Callan in Kentucky, where a similar protective area had been set up.

Six years after the breaking story of the Genetics Council and their horrors, and still there was no resolution. The monsters still practiced their evil, and finding and destroying their Labs was becoming harder each year. Aiden often feared that it would never end.

"Aiden." Dr. Armani stepped from the shadows of the night, joining him on the porch.

"She's asleep. Let her rest for now," he bit out, his body tensing at the thought of Charity being awakened by yet another scientist set on more experiments.

A sigh broke the night. Regretful, yet tinged with mockery.

"I never knew how selfish you could be," she snorted. "I thought you were more the beta type. Where did you hide all these alpha tendencies over the years?"

He crossed his arms over his chest as he leaned against the rough wood of the cabin and stared at her. He was the damned security expert here, what made her think he didn't know how to fight?

"Even genius doctors can be wrong, it seems," he said as though in regret. "I'm sure you'll survive the mistake, though. This time."

She grunted in disbelief. "I need to see her when she wakes up. You know that. I would have preferred to have seen her before you mated her."

"We've discussed this." He tensed as he watched her. "She's not strong enough for more tests."

"I need samples, Aiden. I don't need her body to run the preliminary tests. If she conceives, then your opinion won't matter. Charity knows the score here. When she's more herself, you won't be able to stop her from coming to me."

Aiden bared his teeth at her statement. "You forget, Armani, she is in my cabin, in my care. My mate. She will do as I say."

Armani smiled. Just like that, her teeth flashing in the dark as she sat down slowly in the wide, rough wood chair he had made weeks before. She crossed her legs casually, adjusted her light jacket and regarded him with a mocking glitter in her gaze.

"How the mighty will fall," she sighed sarcastically. "The male mind truly amazes me. The male Breed mind astounds me. What makes you think you can stop her, Aiden? Will you tie her to your bed?"

"If I have to." He wanted to snarl, but he knew exactly how cutting the little woman could be. He had no desire to be on the wrong end of her cutting sarcasm.

She shook her head sadly. "Charity is well aware of the importance of what's going on here. Trust me, Aiden; you can't control her just because it's your wish to do so. She's stronger than that."

"I won't argue with you, Armani," he growled, careful to keep his voice low.

"Aiden, I have never considered you a stupid man. Don't start playing the role now." Her voice was cold, lethal in its sarcasm. "Not just Charity's survival, but the survival of your race depends on her at this point. Don't let your possessive instincts destroy the good that came of what they did to her. She would only hate you for it."

"And how do you know this?" he bit out. "You have no idea who or what she is."

"Ah, and here is where you show your ignorance once again," she sighed in regret. "Charity was, from the very beginning, a plant within the Council, Aiden. A very well hidden mole whose job it was to keep a careful accounting of everything that went on, day by day. All the tests, all the results. How do you think we've gained the information we have so far?"

Aiden's eyes narrowed in suspicion. "Who is this 'we'?" he asked her carefully.

She sighed again. "Do you think I am the only doctor who turned down the Council and suffered for it? There were several of us. You know how hard I've worked, Aiden, for your people. There are others who have worked with me."

"Why didn't you mention this before?" he asked her coldly. "This information seems rather convenient, Armani. More of a carefully prepared lie than any hidden truth."

Yet, hadn't Charity told him that it had been she who had contacted the journalists six years before? She had finally been caught in her deceit against the Council while helping the Winged Breeds. She had been in three of the Labs the Wolf Breed Enforcers had received information on, only to escape with the scientists before they could be caught. She had been in several of the Labs that freed Feline Breeds had sworn she had aided them at, in various ways.

He cursed. A low, vicious sound that grated on his own ears. Armani's chuckle didn't help the anger growing inside him.

"The fun part in dealing with judgmental assholes, is watching them fall when the truth finally hits them. Welcome to the real world, Aiden. Let's see, you've hated and reviled your mate for six years, and still you haven't even questioned how she came to be your mate. Or if she is even truly your mate. Have you even considered thinking past your dick yet?"

The woman had an evil mouth.

"She is my mate."

"Yet days ago you stood before me and said quite the opposite." She tilted her head as she watched him knowingly. "What changed your mind?"

"Does it matter?" he snapped out.

"Actually, it does. Let me tell you what I know, that you are unaware of, Aiden." She held up one hand and began counting down. "Number one; six years ago, to save your worthless hide, a virgin went to her knees and forced your erection when you would have died instead. In doing so, to hide the sudden swelling beneath her hands, she was forced to swallow your semen. The change in her body began days after. I have all the tests she ran on herself carefully documented. You didn't mark her, so the saliva where the Breed hormone is more prevalent didn't create the same effects Faith had from Jacob. But your semen created changes in Charity that were not apparent in Faith until after her mating with Jacob, and her ingestion of…"

"Dammit, I don't need to hear about my sister's sex life." He pushed his fingers through his hair, trying to fight the knowledge that they were trembling.

"You are missing the point," she sighed in exasperation. "The point is, certain changes begin with certain sexual passages. Faith was merely in heat for six years. Uncomfortable, at times painful, but Charity has gone farther than this.

"The hormone in your semen reacted in an entirely different way. I won't get too technical on you, as I'm certain you wouldn't understand," she said, her tone superior, knowing. "But the fact of the matter is, she was the perfect specimen for the Council, because her body already had your

DNA infecting her, slowly, too slowly, shaping itself and her ovaries, to prepare her to accept your unique sperm."

"Get to the fucking point," he snarled. He was sick of the lesson in biology and her careful sarcasm.

"The point is," she said with heavy patience. "The scientists found a way to advance the ovarian change. Her eggs must be compatible with your sperm to breed. To this point, neither my colleagues nor myself have figured out a way to do this. Charity's body holds the answers. To help your sister and your Pack Leader's mate, we must know those answers, Aiden. Charity knows this, the rest of us know this, now you must accept it."

"They hurt her," he said softly, unable to still the rage that climbed inside his body at the thought of it. "She nearly bled to death in my arms, whispering of rest. She sleeps now as though she hasn't slept in years."

"She hasn't, Aiden." Armani's voice was now filled with regret, with compassion. "She has worked tirelessly to help others, even though she knew time was running out for her. Her body was making demands she couldn't answer, and the Council was growing more suspicious of her. Now that she's free, you won't be able to control her; you won't be able to bind her. You have no idea the nature, or the training of the woman you have taken. But I trust it will be amusing watching you learn."

She stood to her feet then, her dark eyes glittering from the rays of the moon, mockery lining her expression.

"You're too smug to suit me," he bit out. "What are you not telling me, Armani?"

She shrugged slowly. "There are some things, Aiden, that you must find out for yourself. I look forward to watching you struggle through it. I expect it to be amusing."

"You find too much amusement at my expense," he grunted in disgust.

Her laughter was light, amazingly feminine. "I must find my pleasures, small though they are, where I can. I gave up my fiction fetish for this practice," she growled irritably. "I should be amused somewhere."

She moved away then, obviously finished with him.

"Armani," he called out softly.

She paused, glancing over her shoulder questioningly. "I pity you should a Breed mate with you. You may find we're a bit more intelligent than you give us credit for."

"I never imagined you weren't, Aiden." Her smile was less than comforting. "I'm just waiting on you to prove it. As for a breeding; ah well, we will see should it happen, perhaps. We shall see."

She turned back and walked away from the cabin slowly. Her shoulders were stiffly straight, her stride determined, though not hurried. A grin edged his mouth. Damn, he wanted to be there should it occur that she did mate with another Breed. Watching the doctor fall would be more than amusing.

Chapter Fifteen

ℬ

Charity came awake slowly, for the first time in more months than she could recall there was no pain, no racking shudders twisting through her body. But the depths and severity of the arousal had changed. What had once been agony was now a deep-seated compulsion.

Behind her, Aiden slept deeply. His arm was wrapped around her waist, keeping her back locked to his chest, his body sheltering hers. His heat surrounded her, warming her. That cold core of agony that had once been lodged in the very depths of her midsection was no longer there. Instead, heat burned.

She could feel the arousal tingling over her body. Like starvation, or an unquenched thirst, she couldn't convince it to ease. There, of course, had to be a scientific reason for the change, she thought, concentrating on the clinical rather than the physical aspects of the changes overwhelming her. Which meant she needed a lab. She needed blood work, vaginal and saliva samples; the list went on. If Nicole Armani were here with the Breeds, then she would have a lab. She would have the supplies and the equipment needed for the tests.

"Do not move." Aiden's voice was husky and deep as she prepared to do just that.

Charity bit her lip as she felt his breath fan over the tender wound at her shoulder. When she felt the long canines bite into her flesh the night before, she had expected to awaken in more pain than she had started out with. The wound wasn't painful. Rather it was sensitive, receptive to his lightest breath and aching for a deeper caress.

She fought to keep her mind distant from his touch as his hands stroked the clenching muscles of her abdomen, easing the ripples in her womb. She needed to keep as much information as possible in the forefront of her mind. The changes overwhelming her once again were varied and intense. The pain was gone, but she didn't like the sensations that had moved in instead.

She closed her eyes as she fought her response to him. His cock was swelling along her buttocks now, thick and hard. The thickness of the Breed cock was overwhelming anyway. Talk about being packed. It had taken both hands to wrap around it in the Lab, and hiding the fist-sized knot that had risen halfway in the shaft had nearly been impossible.

What it had done to her cunt amazed her, even now. She should have ruptured. Should have been so filled with him that she was damaged forever. Instead, the overly sensitive tissue of her cunt had relaxed, eased, accepted the possession rather than tearing in protest.

"You're thinking too hard," he whispered at her ear. "I remember that look on your face, Charity. As though your are deciphering a particularly difficult puzzle."

Her eyes opened, her head tilting to glance at him as he watched her from behind her shoulder.

"You used to watch me?" It had been so long ago, but she thought she remembered every detail of their time in those damned Labs. "I never saw you watching me."

"I didn't want you to see." He lowered his head, his tongue swiping over the wound at her shoulder.

Charity couldn't control the shudder that worked over her body. Oh, that felt good. Better than good. It was almost climactic, almost a sexual act itself. She bit her lower lip, fighting the moan that would have escaped her throat.

"Why?" she asked breathlessly. "Why didn't you want me to see?"

"If you had thought I was watching you, you would have changed," he breathed at her ear, his voice smoky, rough with arousal as his cock heated her backside. "I wanted you to react naturally. I wanted to see your expressions, see the myriad emotions that would chase across your face when you thought no one was looking."

Charity whimpered in longing as he turned her more fully to her back. He leaned over her, his silvery eyes gleaming with sexual intent as his hand stroked her tight abdomen almost absently.

"Every time I looked at you, all I could think about was fucking you," he said ruefully. "Do you have any idea how hard it was to control my body? My need for you? Each drug injected in my body made me weaker, took more strength to fight. I cannot tell you the times I nearly lost all control."

Her eyes widened in surprise, then in shock as his palm slid between her thighs. Charity couldn't halt her whimper of desire. She lifted to his touch, her thighs falling open of their own accord, giving him easier access to the flesh he now cupped in his hand.

There was so much to do. So many things she needed to make sense of, to find the answers to, yet her mind was fragmented, her body's demands so intense, so desperate, she couldn't hold onto the sensibility needed to probe into the puzzle before her.

"So lose control now," she whispered heatedly. The feel of his hand between her thighs, his fingers probing into her creamed slit, was driving her insane.

Practical thought was merely a whisper of a memory of what she should do. The heavy ache in her body was a demanding scream for what she better do. She needed him, every hard inch burrowing inside her clenching cunt.

His lips quirked slowly, his eyes darkening as he watched her closely.

"I can still see your mind working," he whispered, his voice thick with amused patience. "As though you are cataloging and filing away each response, each sensory reaction. I don't like this clinical side you possess, Charity."

"Who can think like this?" She licked her lips, desperate for his kiss. "Trust me, Aiden, my mind is completely on you."

"Oh, I have no doubts there," he said gently, his fingers strumming against her wet, inner lips. He was teasing her, deliberately, knowingly. "Yet a part of you is watching all this, clinically dissecting each touch, each sensation, as though it were no more than an experiment."

His eyes flashed for a second with anger before it was carefully hidden, as though his knowledge of her attempts to reason out why and what caused such reactions angered him.

"What more can it be?" she asked him, watching him, not bothering to hide the conflicts within herself. "We aren't mates, Aiden. Not as you think we are. It's the drugs…"

"Like hell it is," he snarled. "Do you think when the drugs are out of your system, that you will be free of me? That before the drugs you weren't destined to react to me this way? You are fooling yourself, Charity. You know this."

She breathed in roughly as his fingers moved suddenly, parting her, pressing deep inside her. She shuddered in reaction, her pussy rippling in response.

"You grew wet for me before the drugs," he charged, staring down at her, daring her to deny it.

"It was only lust," she cried out. "Lust and some measure of caring, of hope that you would survive."

"You lie." She watched him warily as he bit the words out with enough force to cause the primal, instinctive growl to echo through the room. "Do you think, Charity, had I marked you before the drugs, that you would have escaped this need for me?"

"All we have to do is find a cure." She arched uncontrollably, her thighs clenching on his hand as his fingers moved gently inside her.

That gentleness was so at odds with his expression that she felt held on an edge of fear and excruciating pleasure.

"A cure?" he asked her carefully. "Do you believe there is a cure for this, Charity?" His fingers moved, pulling back, then plunging forcibly inside her once again.

Charity couldn't halt the scream that escaped her throat, or the pleasure that ripped through her body. Tiny fingers of electric energy stroked through every nerve ending. Her cunt spasmed around the two broad fingers as the hard caress drove her ever closer to the brink of climax.

"Aiden, don't torture me this way." She shivered, feeling his fingers inside her, stretching her, preparing her.

He leaned closer as she watched him, his expression tight, angry and aroused. He bent to her until his lips were almost touching hers, tempting her until she licked her lips in anticipation.

"Take my tongue as you did the last time, Charity," he whispered. "Show me how desperately you want me."

As she had last time, sucking it, glorying in the unusual taste that filled her senses. In a distant part of her brain, she knew she should be wary of doing such a thing. The sensations had increased, had inflamed her senses in such ways…

His tongue slipped between her lips, and before she could help it, her lips closed over it, her tongue stroking it back as she suckled it into her mouth. She tasted a burst of sweet spice in her mouth, a summer rainstorm, a fiery shock of need that completely overwhelmed her.

Her arms went to his shoulders, her nails gripping at his flesh as he kissed her. Carnal, greedy, his lips moved over her, his tongue stroking hers even as she fought to draw more of the incredible taste into her mouth, her senses.

The arm beneath her shoulder dragged her closer as his head tilted to deepen the possession of her mouth. The hand between her thighs worked her pussy into a furious flame of need. The sounds of moist thrusts and her strangled moans mixed with his hard groans, echoing around her in a heady symphony of hunger.

When he tore his mouth free of her, she cried out in longing, reaching for him, desperate to experience the mix of fiery temptation and sweet longing she could literally taste against her own tongue.

"You're killing me," he groaned, his lips moving along her jaw to the sensitive skin of her neck, then her shoulder.

When his lips clamped on the wound, and his tongue began to stroke her with moist, hot swipes, she fought to breathe through the pleasure, and the rapidly rising heat in her body.

Her blood felt as though it were boiling in her veins. Heating her from the inside out, burning her alive with the need for his touch over every inch of her body. The light stroking thrusts of his fingers inside her cunt only drove her higher, made her wilder.

"Mate," he growled as he moved over her, his fingers sliding free of her body as she cried out in protest. "Admit it, Charity, you are my mate."

"Yours." She would have screamed the word if she could have found the breath to do so. "Yours, Aiden."

He moved between her thighs, his groan matching her strangled cry as his cock nudged against the wet opening of her pussy. Then she felt it again. The hard spurt of thick liquid warmth. She fought to clear her head, to analyze what it could be.

"Don't think," he whispered, pressing the head deeper into her opening.

She felt it again, felt the rippling response of her sensitive tissue to it. Feathery fingers of reaction seemed to quake inside her, driving her crazy with the hard vibrations of longing that washed over her. She needed him inside her. Deep. Hard.

Her senses were overwhelmed, her body screaming for relief as he slowly pressed in, filling her, possessing her. She was aware of the ejaculations from his cock at alternate phases of the entrance. Each one shook his body, heated her further. She stared up at him, dazed, fighting for sanity and realizing he had no intentions of allowing her to grasp it once again.

"There, baby," he whispered gently when he was seated fully inside her.

His cock nudged against her cervix, feeling as though it were now lined perfectly to receive his release. She trembled, watching the stormy depths of his eyes, seeing the sexual intent in his expression.

"What are you doing to me?" she cried out, her hands sliding to his arms, her thighs spread wide for him, knees bent as she pressed harder into the impalement.

"Mating with you, Charity," he whispered deeply. "Feel our bodies. Will you ever fit so perfectly with another male? Ever feel so deeply?"

Mating her. He was possessing her. Owning her. Tears sprang to her eyes, though her body gripped him with greedy intent.

"Drugs," she whispered desperately, denying his claims. "It's the drugs."

Her neck arched as he pulled his cock nearly out of the clutching depths of her pussy, only to return with a hot, full thrust that stroked her nerve endings with delicious fire.

"Drugs?" His voice vibrated with lust, with anger. "Feel me, Charity. Did the drugs shape your body? Did they shape this hot little pussy to fit me so perfectly? Feel me, damn you." He pressed deeper into her. "The opening of your womb aligns perfectly to my cock, its greedy mouth opened for my seed, and you call this drugs?"

115

"Aiden, please." She was shuddering convulsively, so desperate for release now she felt as though the need would kill her.

As though he could no longer help himself, he began to thrust inside her, hard and heavy, taking her, stroke after stroke of fire as she panted and fought for breath.

"I will prove to you, mate," he growled as one hand caught in her hair, pulling her head back to the side as his lips lowered to her shoulder. "I will prove to you whether it is a mating or the drugs. Feel me, Charity. Feel me all the way to your soul."

His lips covered the mark at her shoulder, his teeth scraping it as he began to fuck her hard, fast. Her cunt tightened around the piston strokes plunging inside it, opening, then clamping around his cock as she lost the last shred of sanity she could have claimed.

Brilliant arcs of pleasure whipped through her body, mixing with the pinching pain as her cunt stretched to accommodate the breadth of his cock. She couldn't fight the pleasure, couldn't fight the needs that tore through her body. Her legs lifted, her ankles locking at the small of his back as she arched closer.

The new position placed her swollen clit in line for his pelvis to caress it heatedly on each downward stroke as she pressed harder into the thrust. Her cunt spasmed around his cock, drowning her with pleasure. It was too good. Too hot. Too much. Her nails bit into his shoulders as his thrusts increased and she felt the hard, deep swelling in his cock begin.

"No." She fought his hold on her hair, but the tugging pressure was just another caress, another sensation adding to the others. "Aiden, please," she screamed out his name as she felt her pussy clamp harder on him, instinctively preparing for what was to come.

Her womb shuddered, her nipples swelling harder against his chest, the blood surging through her veins, harder, faster, erupting...

When her orgasm hit her, she lost herself. All she knew, all she could feel was the agonizing pleasure that pulsed over her as Aiden locked inside her, his cock filling her, his seed spurting inside her with heated blasts of yet more sensation.

The pleasure/pain whipped through every cell, every molecule of her body. Nerve endings exploded in rapture, muscle and tissue filled with ecstasy. Her keening cry as her legs locked tighter around him was rife with her pleasure, with her agony as her womb responded with a hard, breath-taking tremor. It stole her breath, washed over her with an echoing orgasm so fierce, so hot she knew it would change her forever.

"Mine." His growl was a vibrating, animalistic sound at her shoulder as his body jerked with his own release.

A hard spurt of seed shot inside her. The knot anchoring him to her throbbed, pulsed, as he shuddered in reaction. Seconds later, the action was repeated. Each throb of his cock was another pulse of agonizing pleasure inside her body; another pulse of hot, rich semen through her womb.

Her legs slid weakly from his hips, her arms falling to her sides as the swelling inside her cunt began to ease, the hard throb slowly fading away. Aiden's body was a comforting weight against her, a warmth she had thought she would never know. Until he moved.

She opened her eyes, watching carefully as he moved slowly to her side. Echoes of pleasure still trembled through her body, though the torturous arousal had, for the moment, been eased.

"A mating." Confidence surged through his dark voice as he watched her.

Regret filled her, washed over her as a small bitter smile shaped her lips.

"A mating?" she asked him sadly. "No, Aiden, not a mating. A reaction. Nothing more."

Chapter Sixteen

ဢ

"Your feet are doing much better. Evidently the fucking drugs were good for something."

He had fed her, bathed her, dried her, helped her dress, then re-bandaged her feet after apply the healing salve to the rapidly healing welts on her feet the next morning. He hadn't acknowledged her denial of the mating the night before, or this morning.

It infuriated him. He could feel the knowledge of their mating clear to his bones. It was a part of him. His body would not lock to her, the swelling would not occur, if she wasn't his mate. And it had occurred before the drugs had been given to her. He knew and he knew she knew it. Yet still she denied it.

"I need to see Armani," she told him as he straightened before her and picked up the comb he had laid on the night table, beside the bed.

She sat on the edge of the mattress, watching him warily.

"I'm aware of this. Turn around and I'll comb your hair."

She turned slowly, sitting cross-legged on the bed as he began to work the tangles free of her damp hair.

"Aiden." Her voice was tired. Even after the hearty breakfast he had forced on her and the long bath, she still looked too pale, her body trembling at the least exertion.

"I called Armani while you were soaking," he told her quietly, knowing he couldn't put it off any longer. "No tests, Charity. Your body isn't ready for it, even though you believe it is. The arousal and resulting sexual activity is too much as it is. I won't allow you to push yourself further than absolutely necessary."

Her body relaxed, though only marginally.

"Thank you." He heard the relief in her voice and wondered at the clenching of his chest.

"Charity," he whispered, leaning close to her as she trembled beneath his hands. "You have your hopes set that there is a cure for this need you have of me. There is no cure. It is natural. Whether you admit it or not."

He heard her breath hitch as though she were holding back tears. He didn't check to see if it were true, didn't want to know if it was. To know she cried because of the bond they shared would shatter something inside him, he thought. He had somehow, in the space of a few short days, lost the hatred that had sustained him for six long years.

That change alone was abrupt enough. To realize his acceptance of her as his mate, and to have her deny it, more than bothered him. It infuriated him.

"It's a virus," she said simply. "I've tracked it that far. It's triggered by a hormone in the male semen that infects the ovaries..."

"Stop, Charity." He smiled, though with an edge of sadness as he lay his finger against her lips. "I don't have any desire to know how or why it occurs. If you need this to accept what cannot be changed, then I won't fight you. But neither will I allow you to harm yourself in the process. Armani knows this, and she knows to take care. But you will hear it as well. If I see it affecting you adversely, then I will put a stop to it."

She lifted a brow mockingly, causing his cock to twitch at the implied defiance. "I'm weak, Aiden, not stupid."

He sighed wearily. "No, you are not stupid, just incredibly stubborn. That stubbornness makes me horny, Charity."

"Well gee, Aiden, why not just be romantic about it," she snorted as her face flushed with arousal and shyness.

He couldn't help himself. He knelt before her, took her face in his hands and laid his lips on hers. He felt the silken curves tremble as they parted beneath the touch. And he waited. He went no further, just the gentle stroking of lips against lips until her tongue peeked out and stroked timidly at him.

Her hands rose to his shoulders, slid to his neck as he fought to keep the kiss soft, comforting, despite the heat that rose between them. He could feel her in every cell of his body as her kiss stroked the fire in his cock brighter. Finally, in desperation he pulled back.

His thumb slid over the moist curves.

"Perhaps I missed the romance classes during training," he said regretfully, moving away from her as a knock sounded at the door. "That would be the good doctor," he sighed then and headed for the door.

He had promised himself he would allow this, that he would tamp down his possessive instincts, his fury that somehow she would be weakened further. He strode quickly for the door and swung it open. Armani stood there, that damned mocking glint in her eye, a smug smile about her mobile mouth.

"You trained her too well," he bit out as he moved aside for her to enter.

She didn't enter. Instead she watched him closely.

"Before I see her, I want to know if you have taken her anally yet."

Sometimes the damned woman could be too nosy. He often wondered if she didn't do it deliberately, just to keep the rest of them off balance.

Aiden clenched his teeth. "No," he finally bit out. "Not yet."

She nodded abruptly. "Another thing. Physically, how is she holding up?"

Why the hell was she asking him?

"See for yourself," he growled.

She shook her head. "Your opinion first, Aiden. I don't ask lightly."

He breathed in deeply. "She's trembling, even now. She's pale and weak, and the arousal is draining her strength. I worry…" And for that reason he had allowed the testing to begin.

She nodded abruptly and forged into the room, breezing past him as though he was no longer there. Aiden shook his head and closed the door. He knew that as far as she was concerned, he *was* no longer there.

Now, did he leave, or did he stay? He turned and paced to the kitchen table and sat down to wait. No way in hell was he leaving.

* * * * *

"Charity, it's good to see you." Nikki's smile was wide, her black eyes filled with humor and more knowledge than she likely needed, Charity thought as the other woman walked into the room.

"'Bout time you got here," she griped. "I can't believe you let Aiden hold you off that long."

She knew Nikki. She could have easily steamed right over Aiden at any given time.

Nikki shrugged. "Stubborn man. Breeds are not always logical, Charity. Of course, we're talking the male Breeds here. Often the females show a bit more sense."

"How often?" Charity asked in amusement.

"Hmm, sometimes," Nikki laughed as she dragged the chair from the wall over to the bed. "There." She sat down heavily, leaning back in the padded comfort of the seat. "Tell me."

Charity sighed. Nikki didn't have to say what she wanted to know; Charity knew the drill by now.

"Keegan knows much more than I do," she sighed wearily. "All I really know is that the incision made into the womb was to apply the drugs directly and to view certain changes within the womb. They didn't check the ovaries, though, which is where I believe the change is occurring. Those tests were scheduled to begin soon. They were beginning to suspect many of the conclusions I've come to myself."

Nikki nodded. "I have tracked it that far myself, with Hope and Faith's help. The blood, saliva and vaginal samples I took while you were unconscious supports this. The changes are much more advanced in your body, though."

Charity nodded then glanced at her friend. "They had samples of Aiden's semen, Nikki. They had the records from that last night in the Labs. I don't know what's going on, but when they matched the anomalies in my blood to his semen, the injections began. After that, there's very little that I can tell you. I just don't remember."

"The how isn't as important as figuring out what they accomplished," Nikki sighed. "Bastards. They never were very smart."

"Nikki, we have to find a way to reverse it," she whispered. "Soon, before I actually conceive."

Nikki rubbed her brow worriedly as Charity watched her.

"Does Aiden know you love him, Charity?" she finally asked her curiously.

Shock shot through her. "It's the drugs..."

"Charity, even I knew, six years ago, that you loved this man. Does he know?"

Charity shook her head. "It wasn't love, Nikki. It really wasn't. I didn't want him to die."

"Hmm." Nikki watched her for long silent moments. "Okay, let's get started then." The other woman picked up the thick black bag she carried with her as she rose to her feet. "You know what I need, Charity."

Charity glanced at the doorway.

"He knows better." Nikki didn't follow her gaze. "He won't come in here unless we call him, or you cry out." She looked at her. "Can you stand for me to touch you?"

Charity drew in a deep breath as she rubbed her arms. Already her body seemed to be rejecting the very idea of it. She could feel her skin crawling, prickling at the thought of what was to come. Bad memories, she tried to tell herself. That was all. But somehow she knew that wasn't entirely true.

"Is it normal?" she asked cautiously.

"Very normal, it would appear," Nikki sighed. "Makes it damned hard to get any kind of samples at all during the first phases of the mating. Hope couldn't bear to be touched in any way for weeks after Wolfe first took her. Faith had only been marked when I first tested her, so it wasn't so bad. By the time she returned with Jacob, she had already passed the first phase. I'm hoping I can get the samples I need with you, Charity."

"It eased for them?" Charity frowned, wondering what miracle it would take for that to occur. "How?"

Nikki grimaced. "As I understand it, it has something to do with a certain strength of climax. Once that's reached, it eases."

She was hedging. Charity's eyes narrowed on her.

"Keep going," she said softly.

"Nowhere to go." Nikki shrugged as she pulled a pair of surgical gloves over her slender hands. The band snapped against her wrist as she pulled the last one in place. "Though it seems it occurred in those two during anal sex. I'm hoping to find a mate soon who can achieve it the normal way." Her voice was carefully bland, though her eyes were sharp as she watched her.

Charity blinked up at her, shock rolling through her system. "Let's hope we can find a cure then," she said calmly. "Because I don't think the anal thing is going to work."

Nikki chuckled as she prepared the syringe for a blood sample. "Yes, well, we can hope. Though I was thinking more along other lines. Now, let's see if I can get a sample."

The examination was horrendous. If Charity had thought it had been bad in the Labs, strapped to the gurney, her body protesting every touch, this was worse.

Each touch was agony. Like knives scraping the flesh from her bones as Nikki touched her, no matter how gently.

"Easy, Charity." The other woman's whisper, though pitched low, was still concerned nearly an hour later. "We're almost finished."

Charity breathed in roughly as the other woman probed at her stomach, checking the inflammation of the ovaries that Charity knew had occurred. She knew her body, knew the changes in it had to be examined, tested, but she didn't know how much more she could bear.

Sweat covered her body, saturated her clothing. Her fists were clenched in the blankets as she fought the gut wrenching protest each time Nikki touched her. She had started at the mark Aiden had left. A sample of the skin had been taken, the area checked thoroughly as Charity flinched, and the reaction had only grown worse as the doctor moved farther down.

"Charity, I must have vaginal samples," she said gently, glancing back at the door. "Can you hold on just a bit longer?"

"Hurry." She was naked, shaking from a chill she knew didn't truly exist, and terrified she couldn't hold onto her control long enough.

"Stop." Aiden's voice was coldly furious as he stalked into the room, startling the two women. "God damn, Armani, look at what the hell you've done to her. Get the fuck out of here."

"No," Charity gasped as he moved to her, his expression nearly murderous as he went to jerk the doctor away from her. "Aiden, help me." She couldn't stop the shaking in her body, the chill racking her. "Please, she has to finish."

He stopped staring at her in surprise. "Charity, it's killing you. You look like a fucking corpse," he yelled down at her as she flinched in reaction. "What the hell would you have me to do?"

She stared up at him, knowing what he had to do. "Hold me down," she bit out. "Let her finish the exam, Aiden. Please, you have to help me."

Chapter Seventeen

ॐ

Her screams still echoed in his head. Aiden sat on the porch ignoring the silent doctor who sat in the swing on the other end and stared out at the slowly darkening sky. His hands were trembling. He stared down at them, wondering bleakly if he had ever trembled like this? Even as a child he hadn't been a nervous type. His hands had stayed strong; fear had never broken him. Yet now, he trembled like a babe during a hard chill.

Not nearly as hard as Charity had shook, though. And she had screamed. The moment Armani had begun the vaginal examination her screams had torn from her throat. And he had been forced to hold her down, watching her eyes, wild and terrified as her body protested any touch other than his own.

"How long will she sleep?" He cleared his throat, still fighting the reaction that had set in the moment he left the cabin.

"Hopefully, a while." Armani's voice was thick, filled with regret.

"Did you get what you needed?" He couldn't look at her. He was afraid if he did, he would kill her. Then he remembered her tears. The one time he had allowed himself to glance at her, tears had streamed from her eyes.

"I hope to God I did," she finally bit out. "Dear God, Aiden, I don't know what's happening to her. Her ovaries are swollen, her cervix is open as though she were in the last stages of pregnancy rather than the first stages of fertility. Neither Hope nor Faith experienced such pain. How do you bring yourself to take her?"

He glanced at her in surprise. "When I touch her, Armani, her body knows only pleasure. It was your touch that brought her pain."

She shuddered as he spoke. "God, Aiden. I don't know how to help her. I don't know what to do."

"Don't touch her," he bit out. "Until the mating is complete, Nikki, no other can touch her. I tried to tell you this, tried to explain what I felt."

She frowned. "You knew this?"

He pushed his fingers through his hair in agitation. "Not consciously. The thought of you testing her was abhorrent to me, and I couldn't explain why. This was why. I knew instinctively..." He paused as he shook his head. " I knew what it would do to her."

"Faith and Hope have not advanced this far in the change," she whispered as she stood to her feet and picked up the bag that contained her samples. "I don't know what to do, Aiden. Or how to help her."

He shook his head wearily. "There is no cure," he said softly. "She thinks this can be fixed. You think it can be fixed..."

"Aiden, I know it can't be fixed. And I think Charity knows as well. You hear her words, but I saw her fears." She walked over to him, sitting down beside him on the steps of the porch. "When she was in the Labs, the few times I was able to talk to her, she asked about you. Were you doing well? Had you found someone to care for you? Did you ever ask of her? These questions came out in many different ways, but they were always there. And the emotions behind them terrify her."

"It is a mating..."

"No, Aiden. Not like you try to convince yourself. Charity loved you before you ever shot that semen down her throat. She talked of you, wrote about you, and worried herself to the point of tears that you would manage to get yourself killed before the rescue could be pulled off. This isn't a mating for her, it's a loving. And it's that part of it that she denies."

Aiden shook his head. He had known that, somewhere deep inside himself. But whatever love may have existed for Charity must have died long ago. And whatever ability he may have had to live had slowly withered away in his fight for survival. He was too hard, too dominating.

"What of her body?" he finally asked. "I can touch her, love her for hours and never cause her pain. What happened in there?"

She stared into the night as he glanced at her. In repose, her expression was frowning, thoughtful. "It's similar to the Feline Breeds," she finally said. "To a small extent, Hope and Faith have experienced it, though not to such an extreme. Why, I'm not certain, but I intend to find out."

She stood to her feet, stepping down to the ground before turning back to face him.

"She thinks there's a cure, Aiden," she told him simply. "You and I both know better. Be careful how you deal with her, or she may run from you as well. If she does, we may never find her again."

His eyes narrowed. "What are you not telling me, Armani?"

Her lips quirked secretively. "Things that only Charity has the right to reveal to you. Watch your step, my friend, or you be may lose more than you ever dreamed of holding."

And with those words she turned and disappeared into the night. Aiden sighed wearily and walked back into the house, returning to his mate where she slept.

The sedative she had demanded halfway through the exam had made it a little easier on her. The fact that she had continued to demand the completion of it terrified him. She was desperate, certain there was a cure to the chemical reaction that bound their bodies to each other.

Instinct warned Aiden there was no cure. No breaking the bonds nature had laid in place. He had accepted it; refused to fight it any longer. He had fed his hatred of her for years, but once he saw her again, once he touched her, he had begun accepting that he would never be free of her. What had happened in those Labs six years before didn't matter. She had done no more than he would have. She had saved her mate the only way she knew how. And now he would do the same.

No more exams. He paced into the bedroom, undressing, staring at her as she slept restlessly. Until whatever changes her body was going through completed, no one else must be allowed to touch her, to weaken her. The progress she had made in the past two days had been destroyed within hours. She was pale once more, weak and in distress.

He moved into the bed beside her, pulling her into his arms. Her whimper caused his chest to tighten, his throat to close as she burrowed into his body. She was cold. Despite the blankets that had covered her, the fire burning across the room, she felt chilled to the bone.

Finally, after agonizing seconds of body rubbing and burrowing, she found a spot that seemed to fit her. She sighed deeply and settled down to rest once again. Unfortunately, his cock was engorged now, throbbing, demanding the lithe body that had rubbed against it so sensually. He sighed tiredly. This mate business was getting more complicated by the day.

Chapter Eighteen

🔊

"I thought you might enjoy that ride into town today, since we didn't get to go before."

Aiden cleared the table of breakfast dishes the next morning before pulling his chair close to hers and lifting her feet to his lap. She was too quiet, too thoughtful. Too damned aroused. The scent of it was killing him. But first, he wanted her to relax, wanted her away from the compound, Armani, and a bed.

She glanced up at him in surprise. "I was wondering about that. Why do you want to do that? A drive-through?"

He grinned up at her. "To see what I can see."

He watched the play of emotions across her face; foremost was the frustration at his vague answer. Her expressive face had always tantalized and amazed him. Others rarely noticed what he did. A shift of a brow, a certain glitter in her brown eyes, the slight twitch at her lip or the taut line of her nose, which could change at any given moment.

The subtle changes in the muscles of her face would have been undetectable, but for some reason, always drew his eye. It had been the same at the Lab. A careful shift of her body to draw attention to her breasts, which covered the movement of her hands. Or a bright agreeing smile, though the muscles at her eyes tightened, as he had noticed in each confrontation they had.

The differences were varied, nearly undetectable, and most he found endearing. Especially the way her gaze seemed to still, watching him, waiting, her expression neutral, a clear indication she was becoming irritated. His lips quirked at the thought.

"If anyone were going to attack us, they would use the town as a stopping point to gain the information they needed to do so. 'Find your enemies weakness' is always first priority. Agreed?"

"Agreed," she answered slowly. The tip of her nose flexed, like a little twitch. Entranced at the small shifts, he continued.

"You and I will drive through town, perhaps stop at a fast food restaurant for a snack, just enjoy the day a bit before returning. As we do, there will be others watching, checking for oddities, or any undue attention being given us. Then we'll return here as the others wait around, listen to what is said, who is asking questions and what happens."

Her nose twitched again. Curiosity?

"You're using the tactics the Council soldiers taught you to catch their assassins," she finally said slowly.

"Basically." He nodded.

"And they are aware of that." She tilted her head, her eyelids tightening as though she would have narrowed them. "You are underestimating your enemy now, Aiden."

He leaned back in his chair as amusement swelled within him. "Tactics weren't your specialty, Charity," he pointed out. "I believe yours was blood work."

She was offended now. The muscles at her cheekbones tightened, the sunlight from the window could have made her eyes appear to flash with a darker color, but he doubted it. Anger, he believed, was the culprit.

"And yours was arrogance," she sniffed, not bothering to hide the irritation in her voice. "Sure, Aiden, a ride into town would be nice. It's been a while since I've had a hamburger. I could handle one. And my feet are fine."

She pulled them back from his lap now, setting them carefully on the floor.

Aiden stilled his grin, aware that it would take very little to ruin the pleasant mood she was trying to maintain. He wanted her fiery, wanted the blood pumping through her veins, sensitizing her body. He didn't want her angry, though. It would even be nice, he thought, if he could see her smile. A real smile. One filled with pleasure.

"If we could, I would like to stop and buy a few things I need. Some clothes, shoes and so forth. I can repay the expense…"

"The Council canceled all your accounts, Charity," he began.

"I have private accounts," she snapped. "I never used the Council money."

"Charity." He gentled his voice, knowing the blow to come would hurt. "Your personal accounts are intact, but empty. The funds were withdrawn six months before."

She lowered her head, pushing her fingers wearily through her hair. "I had hoped they wouldn't find them," she sighed. "I should have known better, I guess."

"When you're stronger, you will work within the compound here. You don't have to worry about money."

Her cheeks flushed. "I don't need your pity, Aiden. I have other resources. It will just take a while to get to them. I would still appreciate the loan. I will pay it back."

"The loan isn't a problem." He stood to his feet, determined to smooth her way, however he must. "We'll stop at a few stores, get you what you need, but I won't allow you to tire yourself any more than you are already. So don't think you can sweet talk me into letting you."

Her mouth almost dropped open. "I have never tried to sweet talk you into anything, Aiden, other than saving your worthless hide."

"Always get your way don't you, honey," he griped. "Just tie the boy up and play on his weaknesses. How the hell did you know you could make my cock that hard, anyway?"

She rolled her eyes at the question. "You were so obvious, Aiden. Even limp your cock would throb when the drugs were in your system."

"You watched?" He tried to sound scandalized as he snickered in open amusement.

She drew in a deep, patient, sustaining breath.

"You're insane," she grumped. "What about that drive you promised me."

He chuckled then, amazed that he could. The helpless irritation on her face, the flash of forced patience in her eyes, should have angered him. Instead it gave him hope. Hope for what, he wasn't certain yet.

Chapter Nineteen

ဆာ

The early Colorado fall nights were crisp and cool. Perfect for a small fire and the warm coziness of the cabin Aiden had built. The day hadn't been easy. The demands her body was making were even more difficult to contend with. The pain was gone, but the arousal was more strongly present than ever before.

Controlling it wasn't as hard as she had thought it would be. The friendly camaraderie she and Aiden had shared on the drive into town had helped. The bit of shopping she had done had been fun. The new clothes rather than Lab uniforms was nice. But now, as she fought to relax, to prepare for bed, her needs were making themselves strongly known.

After stacking her dishes from a light dinner into the dishwasher, she walked to the living room and the cheery fire that crackled in the fireplace between the living room and the bedroom. She pulled the extra large beanbag that sat against one wall to the front of the fire, and collapsed into it gratefully.

It cushioned her body, allowing her to relax as she extended her legs, pointing her feet to the warmth reflecting from the burning logs. The light gown she had donned after her shower rode to her thighs, allowing the warmth to flicker over the flesh there.

Closing her eyes she reveled in the peace, the sense of safety that permeated the Breed compound. Despite the high fences, the Enforcers and well-trained wolves, there was nothing here to remind her of the Labs and the imprisonment she had found there. But there was much here to remind her of Aiden.

Each inhalation of air she breathed in was scented with him. The earthly male hint of sexuality and lust was nearly overpowering at times. Like now. When her body ached, when she wanted nothing more than to feel him against her, feel him touch her, despite her awareness of what was coming.

Her breasts were swollen, the nipples hard and distended against the cotton gown she wore. Almost lazily her hands lifted. She was alone, relaxed, and she ached. Her hand went to the covered mounds, her teeth clamping on her lower lip as she fought a moan of purely sexual need. Her breasts were sensitive beneath her own fingers, her nipples rising harder to meet the touch of her fingers.

She loosened the buttons that ran down the front of the garment until she could pull the edges back to expose the firm curves to the warmth of her hands. She needed Aiden's hands there.

She gripped one nipple between two fingers, breathing in sharply at the sharp sting of pleasure that pulled a gasp from her lips. Aiden's hands were more calloused, larger than hers, but the fantasy worked at the edges of her mind. Aiden touching her, relieving the growing need building just beneath her flesh.

He wasn't due back to the cabin for hours. She was safe, she thought as she breathed harshly in growing need. She needed relief, no matter how minor.

One hand slid to her thighs, pushing the gown to her hips as her fingers moved to the bare flesh of her cunt. She jerked, shuddered, as a moan tore past her lips.

"Aiden," she whispered his name, seeing him there, perhaps watching her, his eyes growing dark as she stroked her own body.

Would he like that? Would his cock thicken, become erect at the sight of her fingers pushing through the narrow slit of her cunt lips? In her fantasy, it did. She stroked around her swollen clit, feeling the piercing lust that shuddered through her womb at the touch.

Her inner lips were swollen, sensitized from her arousal. The cream from her body coated them heavily, allowing her fingers to slide easily between them until they met the entrance to her gripping vagina.

"Oh God!" She couldn't stop her cry as she pressed two fingers inside.

Her pussy gushed at the pleasure, the muscles clamping around her fingers, begging for more. The wash of sensations was almost agonizing. Heat seared her fingers, her cunt, the lightest stroke into the tight muscles echoing through her body with pulsing vibrations of rapturous pleasure.

She spread her legs further, the muscles of her thighs tightening as the ache rippled from her vagina to her clit. Like a firestorm of erotic torment, the sensations whipped through her body, torturing her with the need for release. She could feel them licking over her flesh with a phantom stroke, edging her passion and her need higher.

She pulled her fingers back slowly, whimpering at the surging intensity before she pushed them forward in a quick stroke designed to mimic Aiden's thrusting cock. Not nearly as good, but she couldn't halt her cry at the flash of piercing need that shuddered through her body.

The heel of her palm pressed against her swollen clit, intensifying the lustful pressure. Her cunt clenched, the empty hunger radiating through her body as she fought to bring herself to climax. It had always worked before. Always, yet no matter how she fought, no matter how deeply she pushed her fingers into the sweltering depths of her pussy, she could find no relief.

Her head was thrown back as she fought for relief, whimpering sighs of desperation gasping from her lips when she first felt the gentle lick to the back of her cream coated hand.

Charity's eyes sprang open, her head lifting, her gaze caught by the hot intensity of Aiden's look as he watched her from between her spread thighs. He was on his knees before her, naked, his dark face heavy with sensuality, his tongue reaching out to lick her again. A forceful lick accompanied by a growl that seemed to vibrate through her hand, into the hungry depths of her pussy.

"Do you know just how fucking beautiful you look to me right now?" His voice was dark, heavy with lust.

When she moved to pull her hand back, he stopped her, pressing his against it until her fingers sank inside her tight flesh once again. He watched the movement, his cheekbones reddening as hunger seemed to glow in his expression.

"Don't stop," he whispered. "Let me watch you, Charity. Take yourself as I watch."

It was the most erotic thing she had ever known in her life. Watching him—his gaze trained on her fingers, his tongue reaching out to lick at the slick slide of her juices— overwhelmed her. His tongue was rough, hot and greedy as he tried to hold her legs farther apart. His gaze locked with hers as he tried to clean every gushing surge of cream that escaped past her heated vagina and her thrusting fingers.

"I can't." She was gasping for breath, her hips thrusting hard into her fingers as she stroked in again. "Aiden, please. I can't…"

She needed his fingers inside her, stretching her, driving her higher. God no, she needed his cock filling her, overfilling her, making her scream as her muscles were forced to accommodate each powerful stroke. She pushed her fingers deeper, harder inside her then cried out as his tongue stroked between them when she pulled back. The hot tip licked at her sensitized vaginal entrance, the sensation ripping through her body like a tidal wave of fiery pleasure.

"I'm going to fuck you until you beg me to stop." His voice was hard, so deep and rough it stroked over her senses like a ghostly touch. "As soon as I can quench this need to drain every drop of your juice from your body."

He pulled her fingers free, only to replace them with a hard, driving stroke from his hot tongue.

Her hips jerked, thrusting into the stroke as streaking, lava-rich sensations raced through her blood stream, beneath her skin, searing her brain with the pleasure. Her hands gripped the sides of the beanbag, her thighs straining as his hard hands held them spread apart. He slurped at her entrance, his tongue fucking into her hard, then pulling back, his mouth sucking her flowing juices past his hard lips.

"So damned good. You make me drunk with my need for you," he murmured at the pulsing entrance to her pussy before licking into her again.

The mindless need for orgasm began to fill her. There was no shame, no hesitation then, there was only Aiden. Aiden holding her still as she struggled, reached for more. Aiden's tongue stroking the overly sensitive tissue inside her blazing cunt, thrusting past the tightening muscles, probing at nerve endings she never knew she possessed. Nerve endings that exploded in pleasure at each touch, screamed out their need for satisfaction, for relief.

"Aiden, I need you." Her hands gripped the bag beneath her as she fought for climax.

Her cunt, her clit, her breasts—hell, her entire body— were blazing, tingling, her muscles tightening at the cellular level in the quest to ease the delicious torment he was practicing on her drenched pussy. He groaned into her flesh, a sound of enjoyment, of pleasure as her vagina clenched, then drenched his tongue once again. Like a man parched from thirst and having found a well of wet, sweet relief. Now if only he would extend the relief, she could save her own sanity.

"Aiden, please," she panted, her voice weak, breathless, shocking her with the primal sound of desperation. "Please. If you don't fuck me I'm going to die."

She twisted as an agonized groan tore from her chest. His thumb began to circle her clit. It tingled, pulsed. Each stroke was like ecstasy licking at the edges of orgasm, driving her higher. She was thrusting against his fucking tongue, whimpering, crying out at each thrust as her vaginal muscles parted for each forceful entrance.

The pressure at her clit intensified, fed by his driving tongue, his suckling lips at her vagina, his thumb rotating against the tortured knot of nerves. Her cries echoed around her, almost animalistic, begging as she had never thought she could beg. Until his thumb pressed closer, firmer, stroking... God yes... Right there...

She screamed. Stars exploded around her as her eyes widened, her body arching, tensing, locked tight to his spearing tongue as she felt her pussy explode. Her upper body lifted involuntarily, the breath halting in her chest as lightning tore through her body. Bolt after bolt of white-hot heat erupted inside her as she convulsed, her wail filling the room, shocking her, as Aiden jerked his head back and rose over her with a primal growl of possession.

Chapter Twenty

ɬ

"Now, Charity," he whispered as he came over her, unable to hold back the driving need for fulfillment that pounded through his body. "Burn me alive."

Aiden felt the pulse of lubricating fluid from the tip of his cock the moment it touched the wet heat of Charity's vagina. He grimaced, fighting for control. He wanted to enter her slowly, to savor every rippling contraction that tore through her tight cunt. And she was tight.

Another pulse of fluid shot into her. Her body tightened, bucking as it splattered inside her heated channel. He eased the bulging head of his cock gingerly into the gripping entrance as yet another stream shot free. He was fighting for breath now. The ejaculations were almost orgasmic, teasing him with the ecstasy to come, the memory of the soul-searing release when his seed would fill her, soak into her pussy and ease their lusts for but a brief time.

"You're so hot. So hot and tight you make me want to howl with my need for you," he panted as he fought for breath.

Gritting his teeth, he eased farther inside her, amazed at how easily her muscles parted for him, how hot and tight her grip was. Her pussy clenched, her juices flowing, easing his way as he pressed into her. Looking down, he fought the near rabid growl as he watched the plump lips of her cunt flattening and stretching around the shaft invading her. The sight of it had yet another of the ejaculations pulsing from him.

She cried out, her hands moving from the side of the beanbag she lay on to grip the wrists that clasped her hips. She stared up at him, her eyes dazed, unfocused, her face flushed with passion, glistening with perspiration.

"Do you know how good you feel?" he growled as he fought for control. "So wet and tight around me, Charity. I can feel the knot just under my flesh throbbing for release."

And he could. The pumping pressure midway down the length of his cock was an excruciating pleasure as he fought the impending release. Aiden eased in farther, his gaze flickering between her satiny, pink inner lips and her enthralled expression.

The head of his cock was buried inside her, easing through the fist-tight confines of her pussy as another pulse of the lubricating fluid shot inside her. It was agony. It was a pleasure so painful he swore he was going to die as he fought to maintain the steady, though slow pace inside her.

"Charity," he gasped her name as he slid farther inside the tightening, building heat of her cunt. "Baby. You're killing me."

"Now." Her nails bit into his wrists. "Fuck me, Aiden. Fuck me now. Hard. Please…"

He couldn't help it. He powered inside her, his head falling back, a growl ripping past his throat at the brutal pleasure tearing through his body. He was buried in her to the hilt now, his scrotum tucked against her bottom, cushioned and becoming moist from the female juices that had coated the flesh there.

"Aiden." She was half raised, almost in a sitting position, her eyes wide, dilated as she stared at him.

"Look," he whispered, glancing between their bodies as he pulled back slowly.

He heard her whimper and wanted to cry out himself as his cock slid back, dragging against her flesh, glistening with the thick cream that coated it. He pulled nearly free, until only the crown remained.

"Watch, Charity." He had to fight for breath, fight to still the tremors that wanted to shake his body, the need for release that pounded through him. "Watch me take you."

He slid home again. Not so slowly, but not so fast that she didn't see, didn't feel every inch of the cock taking her. He glanced up at her again, seeing the fascinated look on her face, the arousal tightening her features.

"Look at me, Charity," he whispered. "Look, baby."

She raised her eyes; they were wide, dazed, almost black pools of surrender as he pulled back then thrust easily inside her once again.

"Mark me," he whispered, every muscle in his body tensing from need as he tightened his arms around her, pulling her closer. "Like I marked you, Charity. Mark me now."

He thrust harder inside her as her lips touched his shoulders. He was close. So damned close he could feel the knot beginning to form, engorging, preparing for his release. His hips moved faster, thrusting his cock harder, deeper inside her as he felt the delicate scrape of her teeth, heard her whimper of nearing orgasm.

Her pussy rippled around him, contracted with deep hard pulls, milking at his flesh as though trying to suck the seed from his body.

"Now, damn you." He couldn't hold back, couldn't wait. The swelling began, the pleasure tearing through him until he wondered if he would survive it.

Her teeth clamped down on the tight muscle. Not enough to break the skin as his canines had hers, but enough, just enough to release the primal urges tearing through him.

He gripped her hips, lowering her, laying over her, feeling her teeth bite down as he thrust into her harder, again, and again, until the swelling intensified, locking himself inside her as she erupted around him.

The heavy contractions of her orgasm timed perfectly with the first hard expulsion of his seed inside her gripping cunt. Aiden wanted to howl, and almost did as the pleasure overcame him, surging through his body, shooting up his spine and searing his brain with the rapture of it. He couldn't stop. His hips jerked, her muscles tightened, and his seed spurted inside her again. It seemed never ending, the pleasure unlike anything he had known or imagined possible.

The engorged knot pulsed and beat as though it carried life itself. Caught in the vice of her spasming pussy as he collapsed over her, shuddering, his body jerking with each explosion of seed from his cock into her body. His breath sawed out of his chest as slowly, agonizingly, the pressure began to ease.

Sweat dripped from his body to hers. Her teeth loosened from his shoulder, her head falling back as she shuddered one last time.

"Mine," he whispered, raising his head just enough to stare down at her, to spear her with the intent growing in his mind. "Mine, Charity. Always."

She smiled, weak but filled with her own determination, her own stubbornness.

"Not yet," she promised him softly. "And maybe, Aiden, not ever."

Chapter Twenty-One

ಬಾ

The sound was so soft at first that he was certain he was hearing wrong. There was a reason why the bathroom window was so damned small. So assassins couldn't sneak in, and so Aiden had some small sense that he wasn't totally closed in. That one concession made the necessity of bars on the windows and locks on the doors more tolerable. But even there the alarm system should have been in place.

His arms tightened around Charity, his hand going over her mouth to stifle any sound she would make as he pulled her quickly from the bed. Her body tensed but moved smoothly with him, as he pulled her to the floor while shoving his hand beneath the mattress for the automatic handgun he kept ready.

Grabbing Charity's arm with the other hand he pulled her to the far side of the second entrance to the bedroom intending to get her into the living room.

He moved her carefully against the thick fireplace wall, sheltering her with his body and intending to rush her to the other side of the room when he first realized the true danger they were in.

"Coyotes," she whispered. "I smell them."

Surprise shocked his system. He had known the scent, knew well what he was dealing with, but he hadn't expected her to smell the distinctive scent as well.

"They can smell me too, Aiden." Her voice was only a thread of sound. "Leave me here and do what you have to. There's no way you can hide my scent."

"Shh." Whoever it was had made it into the house. He had to give them credit for stealth.

He pulled her carefully away from the fireplace, pulling her across the living room and pushed her quickly behind the thick, oak bar stand between the living room and the kitchen before he moved silently back through the room.

The bastard was there for Charity, and he knew it. The scent of her heat was overwhelming, and would most likely block his own scent. He would need that edge to surprise the bastard and take him down. Aiden didn't want the assassin dead. He wanted him talking.

He moved back to the far arch, crouching low and looking around the brick wall. There he was. Small, very small for a Coyote Breed and moving slowly for the bed. Aiming the pistol carefully, Aiden cleared his throat. Then all hell broke loose.

The windows in the kitchen and the living room shattered simultaneously as the whine of muffled shots began to hum through the room.

"Fuck!" Aiden began to fire toward the front window as he jerked one of the automatic rifles from the gun shelf beside him.

Charity. Fuck. She hadn't made a sound and the bullets whizzing through the house were coming through the window directly behind the bar. He rolled across the floor, the automatic rifle returning fire as he fought to get back to the other room and pull her to safety. Son of a bitch. What happened to bulletproof windows?

As he neared the doorway, gunfire erupted from the arched opening into the bedroom. Cursing, feeling the heat of the bullets whining around him as he heard the compound sirens go off, he returned the fire as he scrambled behind the dubious protection of the end of the couch.

"Charity!" He screamed her name out as the house seemed to rock on its foundations.

He heard her scream his name as gunfire seemed to erupt everywhere. Smoke and dust filled the room, obscuring his vision, but not his senses as he heard the scuffle going on in the other room.

He was pinned down by the gunfire from the bedroom, firing back wildly as he fought to find any opening to throw himself into the kitchen.

"Fucking bitch." The dark male curse sounded from Charity's location. It sizzled in the air as Aiden threw himself from the protection of the couch, firing wildly into the bedroom and living room as he rushed to the kitchen.

A pain filled cry echoed from the direction of the bedroom doorway as he slid into the kitchen.

And then he saw it. The large male scuffling with Charity as another came through the shattered window. He aimed and fired seeing the flash of steel as it moved at Charity's side.

An agonized scream echoed through the kitchen as Aiden moved to pull her from the clutches of her would-be assailant. She was moving fast, ducking then disappearing as he fired at the injured man.

She was too fucking fast. Like a whirlwind moving about the room as the shadowed figured began to twist within the dim, dust filled confines of the rooms. Such quick reaction and steady coordination could have only come from years of training. Who or what had trained her?

"Bastards," she screamed as he saw her rise, a gun in her hand, firing behind him. The grunt of pain he heard as he ducked and rushed for her assured him she had hit whatever she was firing at.

He pulled her quickly to him, then behind him as he watched the window, training the gun at the now empty hole.

"Damn it, I don't need a shield Aiden," she cursed as he backed her against the counter.

The howling of the wolves, the gunfire outside, and the sudden silence through the cabin assured him the danger had moved and the Enforcers had made record time getting to the cabin. Unfortunately, the cabin appeared a little worse for wear.

"Aiden." The door burst open as Stygian's rough voice called out his name.

Lights speared into the room as he slowly relaxed his guard and stood up carefully among the shattered glass that littered the floor.

"Stygian, get a blanket for Charity and my pants and shoes from the bedroom. The room is filled with glass." His feet already smarted from the nicks and cuts inflicted on them.

As Stygian rushed for the other room, battery powered lights lit up the cabin as it slowly filled with Enforcers.

"This one's still breathing," Styx called out as he found the Coyote Charity had shot. The sudden sound of a gunshot assured Aiden the Coyote wasn't breathing any longer.

Aiden grimaced. He had hoped to keep at least one of them alive.

Behind him, Charity held to him weakly, her head lying against his back, her breathing rough.

"You okay?" he questioned her over his shoulder.

"Alive," she bit out.

Aiden grunted. "Beats dead any day of the week, huh?"

She chuckled weakly as he felt her shake her head slowly against his back.

"Blanket." Stygian rushed back into the room. He threw the blanket to Aiden, though he carried the jeans and sneakers Aiden would need.

Catching the covering, he turned and wrapped Charity in it quickly. She was pale, her eyes wide and dark, but she appeared relatively unharmed.

"Let me get dressed and I'll get you on the couch." He turned and grabbed his jeans and shoes from Stygian and quickly donned them.

Making certain the blanket was tucked around her, he picked Charity up and moved swiftly to the couch. First things first. He had to check her out, make certain she was okay, then he would find out just how the hell the Council's mongrels had made it past the perimeter alarms, Enforcers and Wolves. He knew what they were after, now he had to figure out how to stop them. And figure out why the hell there had been no sign of them in town.

Chapter Twenty-Two

ରଚ

"You underestimated your enemy," she muttered as he sat her on the couch in another cabin and straightened away from her. "Coyotes aren't stupid, Aiden. Soulless, but not stupid. The very fact that you aren't being watched should alarm you."

He grunted, which did little to assure her he had taken the point.

"Where did you get your training?" he asked her then, ignoring her warning.

"Does it matter?" she bit out, chafing under his possessive attitude.

He stared down at her, his eyes flat and hard. "Do you want to answer me?"

"Army," she finally answered him bitterly. "That's where I received my scientific training as well. My foster parents were Army. Killed during a terrorist strike while they were overseas."

Her upbringing as well as her training had been unorthodox. Her foster parents had been part of a unique group of scientists working in the Biological Warfare Studies group designed, supposedly, to find cures for some of the unique viral contagions that had cropped up at the time.

But he knew all this. Aiden wasn't a stupid man, she thought. He would know all there was to know about her past. His next words confirmed that.

"They were good people. There was no mention of your training, though."

She sighed wearily.

"They won't stop trying to take me, Aiden. You know that," she warned him again, unwilling to allow him to change the subject.

Dawn was peeking over the mountains outside and the entire compound was on alert. Enforcers were pacing nervously along the walls and calls had gone out to pull more in.

She stared up at him, seeing the savage determination in his expression, the stubbornness in his gray eyes. He was refusing to accept the danger she represented to the community Wolfe had slowly fought to make safe for their people

"Think about it, Aiden," she told him firmly, aware of the half dozen Breeds, including Wolfe, who listened behind him. "The drugs were specifically designed to force ovulation and compatibility with your sperm. When their tests revealed the added Breed component in my blood, they checked their own records and matched it with you. They had samples of your sperm. They designed a drug that would enhance and would speed up the process my body had started…"

"Because we are mated," he bit out triumphantly, as though the ongoing argument over the mating was behind her words.

Charity rolled her eyes as she pushed her fingers through her hair in frustration. Was he never going to give up? He was the most stubborn person she had ever laid eyes on.

"Listen to you. You did not mate me, Aiden. You marked me somehow. The drugs mated me, not you."

His eyes flashed like a mercurial storm, the color twisting and surging within itself.

"Drugs created from my sperm. From my individual DNA," he bit out arrogantly as though the fact that it was he she had mated with made him somehow superior to anyone else she may have been tested for.

And still, he missed the point. The danger she was bringing to the compound was her concern, not the damned mating, drug related or not.

"Goddammit, this isn't about the fucking mating!" she yelled as she came to her feet, clutching the blanket tightly around her naked body as she faced him furiously. "Don't you hear what I'm saying, Aiden? I'm a danger to everyone here. To everything Wolfe is attempting to build. You have to let me leave."

Incredulity filled his expression. "And go where?" He spread his hands wide. "Where else would you be even reasonably safe, Charity?"

She would never be safe, and she knew it. But she wouldn't hide behind the very people she had fought so many years to protect, either.

"And if they launch an all out assault?" she asked him loudly. "What the hell will you do then? They know you've fucked me…"

"I mated you," he yelled back, his voice dark, wickedly sensual with its angry growl.

"They know conception is possible, Aiden…"

"By God, if you haven't conceived yet it's not from lack of trying," he growled.

If she hadn't needed to keep the blanket on her to preserve her modesty she would have pulled her hair in frustration.

"Are you trying to make me crazy?" she snarled. "Stop changing the subject."

"There is no subject under discussion," he informed her arrogantly. "You are my mate, and therefore part of the pack. You are safest here. When you are no longer so weak, you will realize this."

She gaped at him for a moment in amazement.

"Get over the mating stuff, Aiden. They won't stop. How many of your people will die before you hate me for it?" she screamed back at him. "Look at me, Aiden. I won't allow it…"

"My mate. My decision." He crossed his arms over his chest stubbornly.

"Drugs do not make a mate." She wondered what it took to convince him of this. "Do you understand me, Aiden? Not. Your. Mate."

"My mate. My woman," he growled. "My child."

The last word shocked her into silence, but only for a moment. "There is no child."

"Yet." Satisfaction glittered in his eyes.

"Ever."

His brow arched slowly. "Do you think you can deny me, Charity?" he drawled sensually. "Already your body is hot, aroused. Any man in this room can scent your need."

Her eyes widened as she swallowed tightly then turned and looked at the interested men watching the exchange with no small amount of amusement. She felt her face flush in embarrassment as her gaze went to Wolfe questioningly.

"You can?" she asked, humiliation crawling through her body as she faced the men.

Wolfe sighed deeply as he flashed Aiden a disgruntled look. "Charity, it is no different for Hope or Faith. The need is natural. And the scent is very elusive, though very pleasant. There is no reason to feel shame."

"Why should you feel shame?" Aiden questioned almost angrily. "Does it shame you to be my mate?"

She was going to cry. Charity could feel the tears rising behind her eyes, the fear blooming in her chest. The need to do so made her furious. Damn him, damn him to hell for making her cry.

"Moron." Her fist connected with his chest, bringing no more than a frown of confusion to his face and an ache to her fingers. "Are all male Breeds so damned stupid?"

Surprise marked Aiden's face. "Charity, perhaps you need to rest," he sighed. "You're no longer making sense."

"Because you're crazy," she accused him furiously. "Insane. Completely without a clue."

She gave up. A strangled growl of fury vibrated in her throat, giving any breed alive competition in primal response as she stomped around him and headed for what was obviously the bedroom. The open door showed the inviting, turned downed blankets, but the fireplace between the two rooms was a dead giveaway. Thankfully, this one had a door. She slammed it hard.

* * * * *

Aiden grinned slowly as the door closed, cutting off his view of Charity and the furious twitch of her hips as she had stomped away from him. He turned back to his Pack Leader and arched a brow knowingly.

Wolfe chuckled, though he was careful to keep the sound low until they heard the bathroom door as well. Moving cautiously to the empty fireplace, Aiden checked to be certain she had gone into the other room.

"Has she conceived?" Wolfe asked. "Her scent has changed, Aiden."

Aiden shook his head. "Armani is testing the samples now. We should know soon. If she hasn't, then she is in full ovulation. Those Coyotes were too damned determined to take her, Wolfe. I tried to keep her within the cabin at all times. And the windows of the SUV were down for only a few moments while we were out. I have no idea how they knew when to strike."

"The scientists would have some idea of the time table involved in this," Wolfe sighed tiredly. "It would be that simple. She's in grave danger, though, as your child will be if she does conceive. Those Coyotes got in too damned easy. We'll have to increase our security both inside and outside the compound."

"I've put in a call to Satin and her Enforcers. Stygian's group will stay, and Drake and his men are on their way in. We'll have to scale back on Lab searches until her safety is assured," Wolfe decided. "Coordinate the groups and re-assign those Enforcers still in the field. Bring in as many as possible. If she does conceive, then Armani will know how to help Faith and Hope as well. We must move carefully on this. All our women are in more danger than ever before. And they are not just our hearts, Aiden. They are our future."

"What about the Roberts woman?" Stygian said curiously. "She was on the list as well."

"When the others get here, take four men and retrieve her," Wolfe ordered briskly. "We don't have time to move carefully on this. Get her here any way you can."

"Satin's group will be of utmost importance as well," Aiden said softly. "You'll have to make them aware of that and pray she doesn't go ballistic on us. Damn, that woman should have been a man."

"Hell, bite your tongue," Styx laughed heartily in response to this. "That woman's so damned pretty on the eyes she makes my back teeth ache."

"She'll cut your balls off if she hears you say that," Stygian reminded him. "Better guard your goods, boy."

Styx winced. "Damn if that ain't the truth. She might look like a little Barbie Doll, but that girl is pure mean."

"Let's clear out of here so she can rest then," Wolfe sighed. "We'll put the wolves on high alert, and two teams patrolling the grounds at all times, two men outside the cabin. You're in the middle of the compound now, so you'll be harder to get to. Let's pray it's enough."

"Put a team of the wolves outside the compound," Aiden suggested. "Use the most advanced pairs we have and allow them to roam wild. They'll pull in the wild packs and alert us of any danger."

Their affinity with the wolves had allowed them to raise and train select pairs for security purposes. The intelligence of the animals and their natural loyalty, added to the surprising degree of communication they shared with the animals, made them perfect for the jobs they were needed for.

"Okay, we'll head out of here so you can rest," Wolfe sighed as he glanced at the bedroom door. "We'll keep her safe, Aiden. You keep her careful. All the plans in the world won't save her if she doesn't use caution."

"She'll be too tired not to use caution," he murmured as he heard the bathroom door open. "See if Faith or Hope can bring her clothes later. For now, I think she needs to rest."

Wolfe nodded as the other men filed from the cabin and then he followed behind them. Weariness lay about him, and Aiden now understood why. The worry and constant strain of his mate being in distress lay heavily on his shoulders. Accepting Charity as his mate had placed the same strain on Aiden's. Her safety, her happiness, as well as the future of their race were their responsibility. A responsibility that didn't set well with any of their mates.

He sighed tiredly as he heard Charity curse from the bedroom. Her voice was thick with unshed tears, and he knew the worries that would be running through her head. He was her mate. It was his job to ease her. He smiled then. And easing her was so damned good, he thought a lifetime of it wouldn't be nearly enough.

Chapter Twenty-Three

೫

Adrenaline still pumped through her body, the blood pounding through her veins even now, hours after the attack. Fury nearly overwhelmed her as she thought of Aiden and his refusal to understand the danger she was bringing to the Breeds that had taken her in. The danger she was bringing to Aiden. And there lay her biggest worry.

"Charity, I can protect you," he spoke from the doorway behind her, his voice dark, rough.

She blinked back her tears, fighting herself and the emotions consuming her. For so many years she had fought her needs for him. Denied what her body, her heart and soul, told her on a daily basis. Just as she had tried to deny it to him.

She listened as he moved across the room, watched as he came into her line of sight, rounding the bed, walking toward her. His chest was bare, smooth tough skin and hard muscle. His abdomen was hard, tight, sun darkened. And below there, beneath the waist of his jeans, his erection swelled.

She licked her lips, hungry for him, her body desperate for his touch.

"Charity." He stopped in front of her, his lean hips at level with her gaze, and she couldn't resist.

She leaned forward, her hands gripping the outside of his hard thighs as her lips pressed against the tight flesh of his abdomen. She needed to touch him, to hold him, to assure herself he was unharmed.

"Charity." His voice was strangled as his hands slid through her hair, holding her close as she licked at his flesh.

The muscles contracted beneath her touch as he strained closer to her. He was hard and hot, and she was tired of the cold knot of fear and loneliness that had grown inside her for so many years.

Her hands moved to the metal buttons of his jeans, her fingers trembling with anticipation as she slid the first metal disk free of its mooring.

"Charity, you need to rest," he whispered, though his muscles tightened as the second disk slid free as well.

"I need you." She pressed a kiss to the skin she had revealed, her mouth watering at the thought of what awaited her behind the snug confines of the jeans.

The buttons slid free easily, and with his help she managed to push the material over his hips and thighs. His cock sprang free, heavy and engorged, the thick veins standing out in stark relief against the mahogany colored flesh.

He was so thick, so hard, it amazed her that her body could accommodate it. She blew a whispery breath over the crown, watching as it flexed then jerked at the sensation.

"Would you tease me all night?" His voice was strangled. "Do you know how long I've waited to fuck your mouth again, Charity? To relive the pleasure of your tongue against my cock?"

She shivered, his whisky-rough voice sliding over her senses like a velvety stroke of power. Fighting for breath, one hand slid across his thigh to cup and cradle his heavy scrotum while the other gripped the base of his cock. She had no hope of enclosing it in the fingers of one hand, she wanted only to hold the heavy flesh steady as her tongue washed over the flared head of his erection.

Above her, she heard him groan. His hands tightened erotically in her hair, his hips pressing the hard shaft closer to her lips. And still she teased him. Why, she didn't know. Perhaps it was to hear the hard, indrawn breaths of pleasure that echoed around her. To feel the desperate throb of his cock head under her tongue, or merely to have him force her to enclose the bulging head between her lips.

His hands tightened in her hair. She allowed her tongue to stroke over the flared head, feeling the heat of it, tasting the pearly drop of pre-cum that eased from the tip. He tasted tangy, a bit salty, and completely male.

"Charity." His tone was harsh and filled with erotic warning as his hands tightened in her hair. "This is a dangerous game you're playing, mate."

She smiled, glancing up at him as she tongued the tip of the silk-encased steel. He grimaced sensually, his expression taut, his eyes stormy and intense as she savored the taste of his cock. Her tongue flickered beneath the flared head, stroking the most sensitive area as his breath caught. She wanted him filling her mouth, thrusting heavily into it, but she needed him to want it more.

For years she had dreamed of the first time she had taken him like this. Knowing she had forced from him something he had been unwilling to give. She wanted to replace the memory with something so erotic he would never remember that episode in the same way again.

"Enough," he finally growled. "Do not make me force you, Charity."

She smiled as she lowered her lashes and licked again, feeling the rough edge of the heavy veins than ran just under the flesh. Restraining herself took more self-control than she ever imagined she could possess. Watching him, seeing his face become heavy with sensuality, his eyes darkening, his chest rising and falling heavily as sweat gleamed on the heavy muscles had her pussy clenching in need.

She knew the moment he had enough of her teasing. His expression tightened, his eyelids lowered broodingly a second before one hand clenched in her hair as the other wrapped around the shaft of his cock, just above her hand.

"No more teasing, Charity." The wide head butted against her lips then slid smoothly into the waiting depths of her mouth.

Charity's body clenched with the dominant, aggressive move. But even more frightening, she felt a part of herself begin to melt. She was hungry for him, ravenous, and she knew from experience that the aphrodisiac contained in the drugs would have been out of her system by now. Her need for him, his taste, his touch, the greedy hunger for him that tormented her would be natural now. And mixed with the heady arousal pumping through her was a shadow of fear.

If this were natural, then how would she ever leave him? And how could she stay, knowing the emotions she had kept carefully banked over the years were not returned by him?

She suckled at the head of his cock, moaning in shattered desire, fighting to hold onto some part of her heart as she heard his hard moan.

"God, Charity…so good." His hands tangled in her hair further as he held her still for the careful thrusts into her mouth.

Her tongue stroked the rigid flesh as she suckled at the throbbing head. Her eyelids rose, staring up at him, her chest tightening with the pleasure on his face. Sensual and savage, his eyes like thunderclouds as he stared down at her, his expression twisted with almost painful rapture.

Shockingly, a hard pulse of warm, spicy fluid shot from the tip of his cock.

"God…stop…" He tried to pull back, surprise and horror flashing across his face as he held her still, pulling free of her.

"No." Her hands gripped his hips, her need for him so stark, so vital she couldn't bear the separation.

The taste of him was dark, earthy. She had no idea what the pulse of fluid was, but she knew she needed more. Always more. She could never get enough of him.

Her lips enclosed the head again, suckling it into her mouth as another pulse of the liquid filled her. His groan was tight, almost animalistic as she moaned around his flesh.

"Baby," he protested, seeming to tremble before her. His thighs were tight, steel hard columns that shuddered beneath the caress on his erection.

She stared up at him, suckling at him slowly, her tongue flickering over the sensitive flesh until yet another hard pulse of the fluid shot into her mouth and his cock sank further past her lips.

Hunger was a hard knot of arousal in the very depths of her womb. Ravenous, her body becoming more heated than ever before, she began to move her mouth on the throbbing flesh, her tongue flickering over it, working to draw the deep, primal growls from his throat.

The head sank to the depths of her mouth, filling it as she suckled and licked. There was no discomfort, no sense of choking on the thick flesh. Her tongue felt more sensitive, the depths of her mouth experiencing a near sexual pleasure as he began to fuck her mouth with short, quick strokes.

She whimpered at each thrust, greedy for another burst of the sweet ejaculation that wasn't a release, yet shuddered through his body as though it were.

"Charity, baby. I can't control this." One hand gripped the base of his cock, the other tangled deeper in her hair as he thrust against her. His voice was dark, its roughness so sexual, so deep, her womb contracted with the sound of it.

Her nails bit into the sides of his muscular thighs as she fought to hold onto her own control. Her mouth tightened on the surging erection, her tongue stroking it, needing more.

"Charity, I'm going to come," he warned her, his voice tight. "God, baby, stop."

She felt the jerk of his cock as her tongue stroked over the deep pulse of the knot fighting to be free beneath his flesh. She suckled at the flesh strongly, loving the way his breath hitched, his body tightened with each pull of her mouth, each lick of her tongue.

"Charity." Another hard pulse of fluid shot into her mouth as her hand tightened on his cock.

His hips were moving more strongly now as he panted for air, as she panted for air. Her fingers caressed his scrotum, her nails scratching at the silken sac as he suddenly tightened.

"Not like this." He moved back, ignoring her cry, her need.

He jerked his jeans from his legs as she moved to him, intent on finishing what she had started.

"Aiden, please." Her lips went to his chest then lower, moving to her knees, starving for the taste of him.

"Charity. God, baby." She licked over his abdomen and a second later her lips covered the head of his cock again.

And he was hers.

Both hands locked in her hair as her hands wrapped around his cock, her mouth and tongue driving him to his climax. She was desperate, needing to wipe away the memory of the time in the Labs, to replace it with this, something deeper, hotter.

His cock pulsed then as she felt her juices spill along her thighs. Beneath her hands the hard swelling in his cock began, engorging, filling her cupped palms a second before the first blast of his hot semen shot into her mouth.

His hips moved in short hard strokes as his groan echoed around her, hot and filled with pleasure as his seed coated her tongue and slid down her throat. The taste of him was an aphrodisiac all its own. The feel of the hard swelling beneath her hands, the crown pulsing, spilling his pleasure in her mouth triggered a deep, convulsive shudder in the depths of her womb.

Her hands stroked the sensitive, fist-sized swelling that had knotted in the shaft of his cock. Each gentle caress spilled yet another explosion of his seed in her mouth as he groaned weakly beneath the caress.

"Baby, so good," his words whispered through her heart. "Charity. Charity, you're killing me." He shuddered again, his hands kneading at her hair, his hips jerking, tugging at her hold on his cock as pleasure rippled over him.

When it was over, he drew her gently to her feet, holding her as she swayed in his grip. One hand moved to her chin, his thumb running over her swollen lips.

"Mine," he growled.

"Prove it," she challenged him softly.

He smiled. A slow curving of his sensually molded lips as he watched her knowingly. "No need to prove it now, Charity. Soon you will know. But just because you have what you needed, doesn't mean I'm finished with you yet."

Chapter Twenty-Four

❧

Before Charity could protest he turned her, bending her over on the bed, her palms flat against the mattress.

"Perfect," he murmured, his hand trailing over the curves of her rear as he leaned close to plant a heated kiss between her shoulder blades.

"We could lie on the bed," she panted, shivering beneath the caress. He could destroy her equilibrium with only a stroke of his lips. She felt lost, drowning beneath the sensuality of his touch.

Heat flickered through her cunt, her womb, as convulsive shudders racked her muscles. She wondered if she had enough strength left to stay on her feet as his hand stroked beneath her thighs, yet never really touched the needy entrance to her vagina.

She shifted, breathing deeply, certain she would collapse at his feet.

"Who needs a bed?" he whispered as his lips touched her shoulder, his teeth scraping the tender skin there. "I will hold you up, Charity. Trust me." His hands curved around her waist, smoothing over her abdomen, caressing up her stomach until he could cup the firm globes of her breasts.

Charity couldn't hold back her cry as his fingers enclosed her nipples, rolling against them slowly as she began to burn with her own lusts. His loins cushioned her buttocks, his cock resting against the narrow crevice there, heating it, fueling fantasies she refused to delve too deeply into.

"Trust you?" she panted desperately. "Your legs trembled too, Aiden."

He chuckled at her neck. "Smart ass."

She would have replied if he hadn't chose that moment to move, to tuck the head of his cock against the entrance of her swollen pussy. She could feel the broad head sliding against the slick moisture there as he positioned himself for a smooth stroke.

"You decide." His teeth raked her neck. "Hard and fast. Or slow and gentle."

"What?" she gasped, struggling to thrust back against him as he easily controlled her movements by gripping her hips.

"Decide quickly." His voice was a hard rumble as his cock throbbed at her entrance.

She whimpered. Hell, she couldn't decide. She wanted both. Hard and fast and slow and easy, hot and strong and…

Her eyes widened, a soundless cry breaking from her throat as he finally took the decision out of her hands. He slid inside her, working his cock slow and easy into the slick, humid depths of her pussy. Her muscles clamped against the invasion, fire and lightning singing through her veins as she felt the tight impalement.

"Wait. Wait," she cried out desperately.

He stopped, though the primal growl that sounded behind her assured her it was only under protest that he had done so.

"What?" His voice was strained, guttural.

She fought for breath, her eyes closing in ecstasy as she clamped her muscles on his cock, milking it to intensify the heated sensations running through her body.

"Charity." His voice was warning.

His cock was buried halfway inside her, stretching her with a pleasure/pain as a hard pulse of silky fluid exploded from the tip of his erection. He moaned as she whimpered in pleasure.

"Feel that," she cried out, shuddering in his arms. "Oh God, Aiden, what is that doing to me?"

Her cunt heated further, relaxing marginally around the flared head as he suddenly thrust hard and deep inside her. Her hands went out from under her, her cheek hitting the mattress as she gasped for breath.

"Are you playing scientist, Charity?" he crooned seductively at the back of her neck as he pushed her farther up the mattress, tucking her knees beneath her as he mounted her more firmly. "Feel what happens to bad little girls who try to play scientist as their mate fucks them."

He taught her the lesson well. He held tightly to her hips as his cock powered hard and fast inside the greedy depths of her pussy. Stroking her like a living flame, burning her with a lust that left her begging, pleading for release. Her body tightened, ripples of her impending orgasm fluttering in her womb, when he suddenly stopped.

"No. No." She twisted against him desperately as her entire body protested at the abrupt cessation. Her cunt gripped him, tightened as she fought to finish the impending explosion.

"Bad little mate," he whispered at her ear as he pulled back with excruciating slowness.

She could feel the sensitive tissue, overfilled, stretching then aching in protest as he retreated. Only to scream out in need as he began to burrow back inside her. Slow, so fucking slow she knew it was going to kill her. He filled her, stretching the tissue of her cunt, the fragile muscles, with an exquisitely slow push that ensured she felt every minute caress of his cock sliding into her gripping, rippling pussy.

"Oh God. Aiden. You're killing me." She tried to back into him with a quick thrust of her hips that he easily controlled by holding the curves in his hard, broad hands.

"I am pleasuring you," he argued thickly. "Feel the pleasure, Charity."

His cock throbbed inside her as a hard blast of liquid shot against the sensitized walls of her cunt. She shuddered. The heat built inside the tight confines of her vagina and blazed throughout the rest of her body.

"You're torturing me," she cried out as he slid back until only the head of his cock rested inside her.

"What are you thinking about now, mate?" he growled, his breath caressing her ear, his voice strained with his own arousal. "Are you thinking of what your body is doing, or are you feeling what my body is doing to you?"

"Now," she panted, his words making no sense as heat speared through her womb. "Oh God, Aiden, fuck me now."

She was filled with him. In a single hard stroke he impaled her with the length of his erection, searing nerve endings, filling her pussy until the heat and pleasure catapulted her into orgasm. Hard, almost brutal strokes that had her screaming through her release, shuddering convulsively, jerking in his arms as he locked hard and tight inside her, his own release pouring into her in pulse after pulse of fire.

Charity collapsed beneath him, her body still humming with the hard aftershocks of release, weariness settling over her like a dark, comforting blanket. Then she realized it was Aiden's body. Broad and heated, holding his full weight on his elbows, his breaths laboring as another explosion of seed pulsed into her pussy.

"I'm going to sleep," she mumbled, knowing from experience he would be locked inside her for several moments longer. "Tuck me in when you're done."

His chuckle was rough, deep at her ear as he breathed in deeply.

"First you're analyzing our bodies' responses, now you're falling asleep on me. You'll give me a complex, mate." In retaliation he moved, causing the knot to tug within the sensitive, swollen muscles of her cunt.

She jerked, shuddered as the mini orgasm washed through her body, convulsing her womb as his seed shot inside her again.

"Oh hell," she whispered. "God, Aiden, don't do that. I can't stand it. I apologize. I promise."

What else could she do? Exhaustion was like a demon inside her now, demanding her rest. Her eyes closed as she drifted in the satisfaction, the repletion of having him still locked within her, a part of her. She was warm and without pain, comforted inside and out, drifting in a haze of well being.

She was only barely aware of his moving, his cock finally sliding free of her body. Within seconds, before her body had time to chill, he had moved her beneath the blankets, tucking them around her, kissing her brow gently.

"Sleep, love," he whispered softly as she drifted away. "I will guard you better from here on out."

Chapter Twenty-Five

ജ

Charity stepped outside the cabin the next morning dressed in the soft gray cotton pants and matching tank top Aiden had purchased the day before. She wore socks and comfortable canvas sneakers on her feet and found herself amazed at the thought of how long it had been since she had worn either.

She stood at the top of the steps of the small porch and tried to ignore the two men stationed close by. Aiden had warned her before leaving that morning that the guards would be present at all times. For her protection. They were protecting the very person who had brought the danger in on them.

She drew in a deep breath, sitting down on the porch step as she carefully balanced the cup of coffee on her knee. Finding the can of coffee under the cabinet had been a stroke of luck. Another of the few pleasures she had been denied in the past years.

She sipped at the dark brew, barely holding back a moan of appreciation. Rich and fragrant, the liquid seemed to sink into her cells, reminding her of all the small pleasures that had been absent for so long.

The sounds from the compound reminded her of other things. Laughter echoed from one of the storehouses down the graveled path as several men joked and talked while they unloaded a pickup filled with supplies. Farther down a group of men and women were training in one of the grassy areas. Grunts and groans and general laughter accompanied their exertions.

In the Council Labs there had never been laughter. Training was a fierce "do or die" exercise. If you didn't excel there were punishments awaiting that defied description. Charity closed her eyes, remembering well the screams of pain that resulted from those punishments. Their lives from birth hadn't been easy. And more died than ever survived the rigorous life they had been condemned to. The evil that was the Council knew no mercy, either, for their creations or for their employees.

The sound of a vehicle moving from the other end of the gravel path drew her attention. She turned her head, watching with a smile as Nikki pulled up in a small, canopied golf cart-type vehicle. She stepped from the vehicle and walked to the porch with a welcoming smile.

"That coffee is very bad for you." The cup was plucked from Charity's hand and in the same movement Nikki lifted it to her own lips and finished it off quickly. "There, no more of that bad stuff for you."

Charity blinked at her in surprise.

"Damn, Nikki. You know how long it's been since I've had coffee?" she asked her mildly, though she was more than a little upset at having her treat stolen so cavalierly.

"I would say close to six years." Nikki sat down on the edge of the porch, turning to face her, her dark face thoughtful, her eyes glittering with amusement. "I bet you stopped about the time the effects of Aiden's hormone hit your system."

Charity grimaced, remembering exactly why she had quit. The caffeine seemed to make everything worse.

"It should be safe now," she grunted. "Or at least easier to control."

"Because you're getting fucked?" Nikki arched a brow as Charity felt her face flush with heat. "Don't bet on it, sugarpie. Faith still has terrible side effects from it. She had to cut it out completely. I think Jacob is faltering under that strain."

The grin that shaped her lips was filled with amusement.

"So, no coffee too, huh?" she sighed, watching her friend closely. "You finished running the tests?"

"No conception yet. But we have some definite changes going on here, Charity. Changes the others aren't experiencing yet. Your ovaries are enlarged, the breed hormone is stronger now than it was when I did the initial blood tests in the field hospital. I would guess ovulation is beginning. It shouldn't be long now."

Charity bit her lip nervously at that information.

"Do you think compatibility will occur?" she asked her worriedly. She wasn't ready for a child. Wasn't ready to be bound that much tighter to Aiden during such a dangerous time.

Nikki sighed. "I need to get into the ovaries. But Aiden and Wolfe have expressly forbidden this. I could steal the egg forming and test it. This would give us the answers to compatibility, and in your case, the time you need to accept whatever is between you and Aiden."

Charity watched the other woman in surprise. "Why would they forbid such tests?"

Nikki leaned back against the post behind her, watching Charity carefully.

"Because of the Council and their tests. Remember, Charity, they have been free for only a short time. For some, only a matter of months. Many of them still have nightmares; many others are still adjusting to freedom and the lack of Council restrictions. They have no desire to experience the tests again," she said reflectively. "It is often painful to watch them adjusting after a lifetime of hell."

Charity swallowed tightly. The six months she had spent as their prisoner had been hell on earth. She clearly understood how they felt. But this was her body, her decision.

"How quickly could you do the procedure? You would have to sedate me…"

Nikki shook her head negatively. "The sedative could change the outcome of the tests, make them false. The procedure would have to be done free of anesthetics in your system."

Charity inhaled roughly, remembering the exam days before. "I don't think I can stand it, Nikki. The pain is excruciating. "

"Another puzzle." Nikki frowned. "I cannot figure that one out, Charity. There is nothing in your system, no reason why you should have such an aversion to any touch but Aiden's. To a point, Faith and Hope were the same. The Feline Breeds have experienced this, but conception occurs quickly in them, without drugs or hormonal treatments. From what I've learned the last few days, you are in the final stages before conception. If we do this, it must be done quickly."

Charity turned away from her, staring across the compound as she focused on the mountains outside the high walls. She shuddered at the thought of attempting such a procedure without a sedative. The pain was terrifying.

"I don't know if I can do it," she whispered. "I know I can't, Nikki. You have to find a way to sedate me."

Silence stretched between them. "Let me run a few more tests then," she sighed. "I need to be certain, Charity, that I can chance a clear result on the ovum. Otherwise the test will be useless. We'll get in enough trouble just doing it." She sighed mockingly. "To think, I gave up a nice little cushy government job to follow these Breeds. How dumb was that? They are much too stubborn."

Charity gave the other woman a knowing look. She knew well her friend's dedication and affection for the Breeds she worked with. As she started to reply a shrill alarm blasted through the compound, imperative, shrieking in its loud demand.

"In the cabin." Nikki jumped up, pulling at her shirt as the two guards rushed around her.

"Inside, Ms. Dunmore." The automatic rifles were raised in readiness as Nikki dragged her into the open door of the cabin followed by the guards.

"What is it?" Charity bit out as the door slammed behind them, the guards moving to the kitchen and living room windows to peer outside them with narrowed eyes.

"Fly by," Nikki bit out. "We've been getting them with increasing regularity."

Charity moved to the other side of the window, peeking out carefully.

Jeeps were racing through the compound, several with mounted guns and rocket launchers. It was like a war zone now. Men and women raced through the compound as the sound of heavy aircraft coming in low began to vibrate through the cabin.

"Council?" she asked the guard worriedly.

"Mongrels," he bit out. "They have hired guns now. Wolfe, Jacob and Aiden are under constant threat."

Charity turned back to Nikki. "What is he talking about?"

"Mercenaries, Charity," she said softly. "We can't trace them to the Council, but we know well who is behind it. Don't worry, Aiden would have called in our government reinforcements the moment the aircraft hit the radar screens."

Chapter Twenty-Six

ℬ

The sound was coming closer. The hard, pulsing beat of a jet-powered helicopter seemed to echo through the frame of the house.

"Do they attack?" She could feel her heart throbbing in her chest, fear racing through her blood stream.

"Sometimes. Get back from the window. If there are sharp shooters watching for you, you'll make too easy a target." Charity jumped back before the words were out of his mouth.

She stared at Nikki across the room, seeing the other woman's concern.

"They rarely attack in the daylight," she said carefully. "They're getting desperate."

The words were no sooner out of her mouth than the cabin trembled as a hard, shocking explosion sounded outside.

"They hit Wolfe's cabin!" the guard yelled furiously. "Sons of bitches. They hit Wolfe's cabin."

"Hope," Charity breathed out desperately as she turned to the guard. "Give me your fucking weapon. Get out there and see if they need any help. I don't need a damned babysitter."

"Charity, stop." Nikki moved quickly to her, then stumbled as another blast rocked the building. "We have to get to the Labs. The underground shelter there will protect us."

"What are they doing?" Charity was enraged, furious. She could hear the screams outside, the sounds of returning fire. "We have to get to Hope, Nikki."

"They are trying to draw you out," Nikki yelled furiously. "Don't worry about Wolfe and Hope. Wolfe knows how to protect his mate. I promise you, our best men, as well as Wolfe, are guarding her now."

"They're turning. Get the hell out of here, they're heading in our direction," the guard at the window called out as he turned and jerked the front door open quickly.

"The Labs," Nikki called out. "We'll only be safe in the Labs."

"Come on." He grabbed Charity's arm, rushing her for the door. "They took out Wolfe and Jacob's cabin and are heading back."

Charity moved between the guards, making no move to question them or to delay their plans. She was aware of Nikki behind her and the sound of the helicopter as it moved in once again.

"Sons of bitches have to have a plant," one of the guards cursed as he rushed her from the porch and under the cover of the trees that grew alongside the gravel path. "Let's move."

The helicopter was moving in faster now. Charity could hear it, the motor throbbing, rotors beating in time to the desperate throb of her own heart. The guards were running beside her, checking behind them often, as curses sizzled from between their lips.

One minute she was running with him, the next she felt as though some unseen hand had picked her up, throwing her through the air as another explosion sounded behind them.

She heard herself scream a second before she hit the ground, the air expelling from her body with the force of her landing. She lay still, fighting to breathe, blinking against the blinding pain that attacked her body.

"Move." She was picked up unceremoniously and hauled backward at the exact instant that a spray of bullets littered the gravel where she had lain.

All hell was erupting around her as she fought to breathe, to make sense of the screams echoing through the air. She looked around then, gasping, as her heart thumped in fear.

The guards were unconscious or dead—she wasn't certain which—and moving in carefully were three large males, their scent unfamiliar, their faces hard, intent.

"Nikki!" she yelled as she backed away from them, glancing behind her desperately then coming to a stop once again.

Nikki was dazed but standing, held upright by two other men, their shadowed faces determined.

"Come with us, and you won't be harmed." She turned quickly as the obvious leader spoke up. "No, Ms. Dunmore. Don't make me force you."

She would have fought, but there were five and Charity knew there wasn't a chance she would escape unharmed.

"You'll kill us anyway," she screamed as another explosion rocked the ground. Then she gasped in horror as he smiled. The canines were curved, gleaming, proof that the Coyotes had finally found her.

"I don't want to hurt you, but I will if I must," he snarled. "Believe what you will for now, but you will come with us."

Gloved fingers gripped her arm, pulling her to the hole that had been blasted into the compound wall. Fear snaked through her belly as her body protested the touch, sending flares of pain radiating through her. Thankfully, as he pushed her forward, he released the grip he had on her.

Charity prayed that somewhere, somehow Aiden was close by. Prayed he was safe. She could feel her cheeks, damp with tears, with desperation, as she glanced back at Nikki, hearing the other woman's vicious curses. She was frightened. Nikki rarely cursed unless the fear overcame her natural restraint. That fear increased her own.

They were rushed through the break in the wall before being pushed quickly into a waiting jeep. Within seconds the vehicle was tearing away from the compound beneath the cover of the thickly growing pines as the helicopter swooped in for another pass at the compound.

"I hope you all fry in hell," Nikki cursed them as they bounced over a particularly rough piece of ground. "I hope Wolfe and Aiden castrate you all."

No answer was forthcoming. The sound of battle receded as Charity fought the rage crawling through her system. Coyotes. They were no more than the Council's lapdogs. How would Aiden find her now, even if he had managed to survive the attack? He wouldn't know what had happened to her. Would he believe she had been in the cabin when it exploded? Of course he would.

She crossed her arms over her chest, fighting the desperation she could feel weakening her. She had to find a way free of this.

"Wolfe will pay you more than the Council ever can," she bit out, knowing the mercenary hearts of the mongrels who had taken them. The Coyotes were known to betray their masters often. If the price was right. "You're making a mistake taking us back."

The driver glanced back, his surprisingly light blue eyes gleaming with disgust. "The Council doesn't own us, Ms. Dunmore, and we have no intention of taking you to them. You'll be returned to your mate as soon as you have accomplished something for us. Now sit back and relax. You'll understand in due time."

Shock left her gasping for breath. He was Coyote. She could see in the curved canines as he snarled, but she couldn't smell the rancid scent that normally emanated from the soulless Breed.

She glanced at Nikki, seeing her eyes narrow, her expression harden as she turned her gaze back to the men in front of the jeep.

"The Council has puppets in many places," she said.

Charity held her breath. The words were simple, but the meaning behind them she well knew.

The passenger turned back to her slowly, his gaze narrowed, intent.

"Puppets have masters. Men play the fools. Breed Law will still yet survive."

And the answer was given. An answer only a handful of men and women could know. An answer that shocked Charity to the core of her being. Breed Law was barely formed. A code of honor so strict, so tightly enforced, that if a member broke it, be he Wolf, Feline or human, then instant death resulted.

"Your Pack?" Nikki questioned. "You aren't Wolf. You're Coyote. Who controls you?"

The smile she received in return was hard, mocking in its savagery. "No one or nothing controls us, doctor, save the code we follow."

"That attack broke the code," she informed him furiously. "You know the price to be paid."

"The attack was not ours," he growled. "Settle back and be patient. Your questions will be answered soon. And hopefully, ours will as well."

"It doesn't matter who attacked, Aiden will kill you before you get a chance to explain," Charity informed him furiously. "You've made a mistake, Coyote."

Broad shoulders shrugged negligently as he turned back to face forward. Nothing else was said. The jeep increased speed as it broke the tree line and bumped onto the main road. The engine whined as gears shifted and the distance between herself and Aiden increased.

Charity rubbed her arms and turned to Nikki, questioning their options silently. The other woman sighed and shook her head. Like Charity, she knew they could only wait and see what the end of the journey brought.

Chapter Twenty-Seven

❧

Aiden stared at the hole in the compound wall, the letter he had found tacked to it.

Breed Law dictated I make contact. I did so. Many times. Now, the ball is in your court. Though, my friend, I have what I needed. Do you? Del-Rey.

Del-Rey. Aiden had heard the name several times by the spies within the intricate network of information he had built over the years. Del-Rey, the light-haired Coyote who had broken away from the Council years before and disappeared from sight. His pack numbered at several dozen, and all hand picked and trained by him years before.

There was a rumor that unlike the Council Coyotes, Del-Rey and his men had adopted an honor system more brutal than even that of the Breeds.

"When were we contacted?" he asked Wolfe, the need for violence tightening every muscle in his body.

Wolfe shook his head, staring into the distance thoughtfully. "There were several messages sent while we were rescuing the Winged Breeds. When I went to answer them, they had disappeared. I haven't tracked them down yet."

"I wasn't told of this?" Aiden growled. As head of security the missing messages would have been an important bit of information.

"You were busy. Hawke's been investigating the problem and I believe he's close to an answer." Wolfe shot him a hard, dark look. "Your mate was more important, Aiden."

Aiden snarled again, the growl that thrummed in his chest was harsh, warning. "And now my mate is gone, because of a few missing messages," he bit out. "Once she's found, Wolfe, I'll personally track down the traitor and exact vengeance myself."

Around them, the compound was organized chaos as everyone worked to repair the damage the attack had reaped. The Air Force had finally made their appearance and blown the helicopter into enough pieces to shower the area with metal and burning debris. But not before extensive damage had resulted.

Aiden clenched his teeth, fighting to restrain the growl that pulsed in his chest. Fury was a bleak, burning pain in his chest. Or was it fury? All he could think about was Charity. Was she hurt? Had they touched her? Made her cry out in pain? He was nearly shaking with the hard edge of violence fighting to be free at that thought.

"We've been betrayed," he said softly. "Those in the helicopter knew where to strike, and when to move in. Your cabin, Jacob's, and the one we moved to in the middle of the compound. Each one was sheltered from their radar and from sight. They knew where to hit."

"No Wolf Breed would have betrayed that information. It had to be one of the soldiers the Army assigned," Jacob bit out. "That could explain the missing messages as well as the attack on Aiden's cabin before."

Wolfe turned, staring back at the action going on throughout the compound. There was only the three of them at the wall. They had arrived in time to watch the jeep disappear over the rise and to find the note attached to the wall.

"She's not in danger from the Council. But why would he need Nikki and Charity?" he asked quietly. "And how did they know when to be here, unless they were aware of the attack coming?"

"There's rumor Del-Rey has a network within the Council," Aiden bit out. "After this thing with Charity was resolved, I had intended to set up a meeting."

Wolfe grunted. "It would appear Del-Rey wasn't willing to wait. Come on, let's get back to the command center. If a message comes through, we need to be certain that we alone see it."

"Finding our spy won't be as easy," Aiden bit out. "When we do, I want him, Wolfe."

"He's not under Breed Law, Aiden," Wolfe reminded him tightly.

"Then I'll do it quietly," Aiden bit out. He wouldn't let the betrayal go unpunished, it didn't matter who it was, or who they were with. Several of their people had been seriously wounded in this attack, and now Charity and Nikki were missing. Breed Law demanded justice. He demanded it.

"We have to find him first." He jumped into the open jeep, waiting on Jacob and Aiden to follow before he put it in gear and headed for the communications building. "Breed Law only applies to those who agree to it, Aiden, you know this. But the betrayal won't go unpunished, I swear that."

The drive to the communications building was a short one. Once the vehicle came to a stop, Aiden jumped from the back seat and moved purposely to the door. The betrayer had to be part of those who manned the radios and computers for the compound. Nothing else made sense.

He stepped into the room, staring around at the men and women working there. Radar, satellite communications, cell phone transmissions, email and radio all came through here. Every man and woman who worked within the large room would have had access to the messages that had come just before they left for South America. One of them had been responsible for destroying them.

He moved through the room, aware of Wolfe and Jacob at his back, watching the others carefully. There were over half a dozen Army personnel. He refused to believe a Breed had betrayed the locations of the most important cabins on the compound. No Wolf Breed alive would have betrayed their Pack

Leader. The code of honor was a part of them, even before the written law came into effect.

"Clear out the humans," he muttered as he turned to Jacob. "I want only Breeds in this room until we get a message. Assign them elsewhere, put them on cleanup duty, I don't care. But get them the hell out of here."

The rage building inside him was nearly more than he could control. The distinction between Breed and full-bred humans had never been so impressed upon him as it was now. They were fighting for equality, fighting to make their way in a world where they had been created rather than conceived naturally. They hadn't wanted to be different. But Aiden felt the differences now more than he had in his entire life.

Not that it was unheard of for a Breed to turn violent. Quite the opposite. But never did one Breed betray another to the Council or to other humans. Their crimes were often against the Council or humans suspected of working with them. A few instances of insanity had pitted a Breed against his Pack, but never to the extent that they betrayed them to the monsters who created them.

Disposable soldiers. This was what they had been designed for, he thought as he sat down in front of the master computer. Disposable. Without value. Creatures designed and created to follow the whims and cruelties of those who made them.

In the eyes of the Council they had no humanity. They were animals, nothing more. In the eyes of many full-bred humans, he knew it was the same. He had seen it in their eyes, in their actions. The Breeds were different. They were animals, undeserving of loyalty or life. Undeserving of his mercy. When he found the bastard who had betrayed them, he would kill him. It was that simple.

Chapter Twenty-Eight

∞

"Have I mentioned I hate caves," Nikki bit out as the jeep pulled into the wide entrance of just that. A cave.

The two men in the back jumped out and within seconds an expanse of concealing foliage slid across the entrance. Charity watched the maneuver with narrowed eyes. From a distance, the fake evergreens would look real and would effectively hide the entrance of the cave.

"Come on." The driver jumped from the front and turned back to them as lights flickered on in a tunnel to the left of them.

"Impressive." Charity gave the driver a hard look as she moved from the jeep. "I bet you can see the Breed compound easily from here."

She had paid attention to the drive as it was made. Several times she had glimpsed the large lake that the compound sat beside as they moved into the mountains. She roughly guessed that with the right equipment, spying into the compound would be easy enough.

No one answered. They were moved quickly, impatiently through the tunnel until they entered a large, cavernous room. There, Charity stopped in shock. It was well lit, comfortably heated and laid out almost like a large home.

On the far side stood several electric cooking rings. Rough wood shelves held an assortment of pots and pans and dry goods. A small refrigerator sat on what was obviously a homemade table. Across from it was a long plank table with simple wood chairs.

Charity was standing at the entrance of what appeared to be the living area, though, benches, a few old, beaten recliners, a couch that had seen better days, and a card table.

"We'll redecorate one of these days." The hard-eyed Coyote glanced at her mockingly. "Come on, through here."

Another tunnel led off to the side. This one was lit by several fat candles that had been set within grooved ledges in the stone wall. Within seconds of entering the narrow walkway, Charity heard the first moan. It was low, distressed and definitely female.

"Shit," she heard Nikki mutter behind her, and Charity silently agreed. She knew that sound.

They entered a bedroom. Against the wall a wide bed had been set up, made from rough wood but holding a large mattress. On the mattress the woman was curled into a fetal position, her arms wrapped around her abdomen. Beside her sat a tall, roughly handsome male, his dark blonde hair falling past his shoulders, his eyes cold and unusually black in his weathered face.

He rose to his feet, the damp cloth he had been holding in his hands dropping to the table beside the bed. His eyes went to the men behind her.

"Casualties?" he asked.

"None. The Council was attacking so we grabbed them and ran before anyone was the wiser."

His broad chest lifted with a weary breath.

"Oh, I'm certain someone's wiser by now," Charity bit out as she moved for the bed and the woman laying on it.

"I hope you at least have some medical supplies," Nikki bit out as she followed. "What happened to her?"

Charity pushed back the long, tangled red hair that lay over the woman's face and checked her shoulder first. The whimpers, the position of the body and the soft scent she detected assured her she knew exactly what she was looking at. She looked at Nikki.

The doctor stood back.

"Who bit the woman?" She turned her fierce gaze on the man who had moved back at they neared the bed.

Charity watched him as well. His eyes were as black as the pits of hell, though his gaze was as cold as ice.

"What does the mark have to do with it?" he bit out. "We're not infected, woman."

Charity watched the tight, sarcastic smile that shaped Nikki's lips.

"Of course you are," she almost crooned. "If what I see is true, you're infected with this amazing little hormone, Coyote. It's really quite astounding."

The Coyote's eyes narrowed. "Explain."

"You mated the woman." Charity wasn't in the mood to listen to Nikki bicker with the Coyote. She was tired, sore, and by God, she was horny. She wanted to waste as little time here as possible so she could get back to Aiden, their bed, and relief.

"Mated her?" he bit out. "Coyotes don't mate, woman. No matter the rumors…"

"Did you swell within her, big boy?" Nikki bit out. "While you were taking her, it's more than obvious you bit her, so I'll assume you locked inside her as well?"

"An anomaly," he growled. "Animal instinct."

"I know the Council trains their Coyotes in sexual conquest," she sneered the term the Council used for rape. "Don't tell me this is your first woman."

Charity listened to the bickering going on behind her as she checked the woman's pupils, her pulse then checked for the brand the Council placed on all its creations. She stilled when she pulled the girl's hair back and found nothing on her shoulders. She moved to her hips, pulling the blanket aside, and still found nothing.

"Charity?" Nikki questioned her actions.

She turned back watching Nikki intently. "She's not a Breed."

Nikki moved then. She didn't speak and, like Charity, ignored the men as she began to exam the woman. She pushed at their hands, whimpering at each touch. She was perspiring heavily, her face pale, her blue eyes dazed as she fought them weakly.

"Son of a bitch," Nikki cursed. "Now look." She turned on the male watching them with a glitter of fury in his eyes. "I've cursed for hours straight. Do you know how mad that makes me? Do you know how mad you are making me? Do you have any idea what you've done? Please, tell me you didn't rape this girl."

Fury lashed through her voice. Charity herself was trembling at the thought as she glimpsed the small bruises on the woman's breasts and arms.

"There was no rape," he bit out.

"Who took her?" Charity turned back then, facing him with Nikki, rage trembling through her body. "It was you, wasn't it?"

"It was." He made no excuses, though Charity had found that few Breeds did.

"You mated her. She's in heat. Does she even know what you are?"

He blinked, his gaze flickering from the woman who moaned roughly on the bed back to Charity, then Nikki.

"I am a Coyote. Coyotes do not mate."

"Well, big boy, either you advanced or you just plain lucked the fuck out," Nikki snarled.

Charity winced. She said fuck. It wasn't good when Nikki said fuck.

She watched the male's stubborn jaw tighten. He looked like a blonde-haired avenger with those black eyes staring down at them, his dark face flushing with anger or embarrassment, she wasn't certain.

"Contact the compound now," she bit out. "She's in advanced fertility and she's in heat. Neither of you are safe because if the Council finds out, and somehow they will, then this woman's life isn't worth squat. Do you understand me?"

"Aiden has been contacted," he bit out, his gaze going to the woman once again. "What is the mating you keep talking about?"

She crossed her arms over her breasts, watching him with an almost rabid amusement. She was mad enough, and just frustrated enough that she was beyond caring if she antagonized her captor.

"She belongs to you now," Charity bit out. "Her body is preparing itself, changing, matching yours enough that she will conceive." Did he pale? "She's in heat. She needs to be fucked. A lot. Almost constantly. By only you. Go figure. You're the first Coyote to mate, and you mated a full human at that. Damn, if you haven't shot some theories to hell and back. And here we thought Coyotes were only good for their stink."

"We do not stink," one of the men behind her growled.

"Was she talking to you?" Nikki asked him sweetly. "We didn't pull your chain, big boy."

Pale blue eyes narrowed fiercely. "You have a smart mouth, woman," he bit out.

"Oh, you just realized that? Aren't you the smart one?" She used the tone Charity knew was reserved for only the most obtuse.

"You wasted your time bringing us here," Charity bit out. "And trust me, Aiden won't be pleased. You better be finding a hole to hide in…"

"There is no hole deep enough," Aiden's furious growl interrupted her as he stalked into the room. Following him were over two-dozen Wolf Breeds, their rifles raised warningly as they stepped into the room.

"Well, looks like the cavalry has arrived," Nikki sniped. "All male and all pumping testosterone. Morons."

Charity sighed. Nikki wasn't pleased. It wouldn't be a pleasant return trip.

Chapter Twenty-Nine

80

Aiden stood in the entrance of a smaller cave farther atop the mountain the Coyotes had taken as home base. The cave was accessed by several long tunnels, then a ladder that led into a natural opening into the floor of the upper cavern. There, within the outside entrance, the leader of the Coyote Pack had set up a long distance telescope aimed into the Breed compound.

"We've been watching you for months," he commented as Aiden focused the telescope with its night vision sight and watched the movements below. "When I first learned that several of your women were experiencing problems similar to Anya's, I started sending the messages. When there was no answer, I grew desperate."

The moving red targets below flitted between trees and natural shelters as they patrolled the perimeters of the compound. Aiden knew there were also several others protected against the night vision sights who were keeping careful watch within the large trees of the area. Both inside and out.

"When did you first realize who our spy was?" he asked, knowing Del-Rey's messages as well as his means of drawing an answer were designed to keep his own identity hidden, as well as his location.

"Several days ago," the other man sighed. "I received information of the attack several hours before it happened. I sent yet another message. Once more it was ignored."

Aiden grunted.

"Were you able to identify the spy?" He wasn't in the mood to play games. He wanted the identity of the man who had dared to betray them.

"Breed Law demands death," Rey mused softly. "Sometimes the answer isn't always so cut and dried, Wolf."

Aiden rose from the sight of the telescope and pinned the other man with a hard look. "Breed Law exists for a reason, Del-Rey."

The Coyote sighed wearily as he stared out into the night sky. "Being a Breed makes us much different from others," he said softly. "I've learned this, as I know you have. Full humans are varied in their consideration, their acceptance and their own codes of honor. To exist in this world we may have to make allowances."

Aiden watched him for long minutes then. The Coyote's shoulders were defiantly straight, his expression resigned. He leaned against the entrance to the cave, staring out as though the answers to their problems could be found there, in the concealing shadows of the night.

"Get to the point," he bit out. He was more than eager to head home and to take care of the problems threatening the peace of his relationship with Charity, and his people.

The other man turned to look at him slowly.

"The Wolf Breed Packs have, in some ways, adopted the residents of the town, trusting them, believing in them and the propaganda of their officials that the Breeds are welcome. You treat it as though it were a place deserving of your loyalty, when in fact the hatred breeding there could eventually be the downfall of the Wolf Breeds."

Aiden took a deep breath, preparing himself for what was to come as he met the other man's gaze directly.

"What have you learned?"

"Many interesting things." He gestured back to the entrance to the main caverns. "I kidnapped Anya outside a Council Lab in Russia. The information I learned from her was rather surprising. There are quite a few groups forming eager to see all the Breeds wiped from the face of the earth. Men whose fathers and grandfathers before them have perpetuated the Race wars of the past have found a new fight. The Breeds will never find acceptance, Aiden. We will always find death no matter which course we take or which land we settle. And the conspiracy against them will begin here, centered around this compound Wolfe builds to protect his people." Del-Rey's voice was soft, consoling as he spoke of yet more treachery, more deceit and death.

"No man is an island, Del-Rey," Aiden reminded him softly. "There are many good people out there, willing to put their lives on the line right alongside the Breeds. We can't discount them. And our numbers are too small to do anything but pray that acceptance will come, in time."

"The Breeds are treading many fine lines," Del-Rey sighed. "And if what I am learning from my own sources are true, the Council will never be disbanded. Their funds are too plentiful, and those who would help them, number too high."

"Who is the spy within our compound?" Aiden asked again. "The rest we will deal with, but he comes first."

"And if it is not a he?" the Coyote asked patiently. "If your traitor is female and well liked within your community, how then will you justify her execution?"

It would have to be complicated, Aiden thought furiously. Why did he expect anything else now?

"The same as I would any man's," he bit out. "They signed Breed Law to work within the compound. Man or woman, they accepted the risks."

"And if they believe their fight is one justified by their beliefs?" he asked. "How do you punish someone for being true to their beliefs? Or to their own conscience?"

Damn it. A philosophical Coyote was the last damned thing they needed. But mixed with his irritation was his own sense of helplessness. A male traitor would have been easy to kill. A woman… He pushed his fingers tiredly through his hair as he leaned his shoulder against the rock wall beside him. A woman was to be protected, cherished, not executed.

"Interesting questions," he sighed. "Thankfully, it's not my call. But she will be dealt with, Del-Rey. One way or the other. Who is she?"

"She is the daughter of the Mayor. She mans your radios and while neither you nor Wolfe are present, she secretly slips information to your enemies through her father. But the woman can be used. She hasn't betrayed you entirely. Remember, Aiden, who made certain Hope and Faith were not in those cabins before the attack. One of my men watched her movements. Watched as she went to each one and drew them to the communications building only minutes before the helicopter was spotted on radar. The Council wanted only one woman. The one most likely to breed. Your woman."

"Jessica," he breathed the name in surprise. The young woman was in her first year with the American Military. He had thought her shy, timid, not the type to so willingly betray the people she had pledged to protect.

"She may even be unaware she had betrayed you." Del-Rey shrugged. "Her father, though, is aware of his crimes, as are many in her family and the town she comes from. Can you kill them all?"

And there lay yet another complication. They had sworn to give each man, woman and child in the world they sought to survive in, a chance. Individually. To trust as any full human would, in the compassion and generosity of the human spirit that they had hoped existed. There had been many who had helped them over the years. Many who had betrayed them. This blow would change how well the Breeds dealt with the town now, and the trust they had placed in them.

"It would be best if you stay hidden here," he finally sighed, knowing that Charity and Nikki were insistent that the woman be moved to the compound. "You seem to be pretty secure. Until we get rid of the full humans working within the compound, then your woman won't be safe, and neither will you. The news that Coyotes can mate will rock the Council. It could cause more bloodshed on the heads of those serving you within the organization."

"They are few," Del-Rey grunted. "But I agree. I will need some time to alert them and have them head for safety. We've grown rather fond of our new home here; we may attempt to stay as long as possible. The freedom of it is much cherished."

There was a world of weariness in the other man's voice. A weariness Aiden knew resided within himself. Their fight had only just begun, and he feared it might turn into a long, bloody battle that the Breeds could ultimately lose.

"We'll head out before daylight." Aiden moved quickly for the entrance back to the tunnels. "Go take care of your woman, Del-Rey. And if you would be so kind as to provide one of your sleeping caverns, I'll take care of mine."

Charity's heat had called to him before Del-Rey had drawn him to the vantage point to discuss the reasons why they had taken Charity and the doctor as they had. Aiden had been in little mood to hear excuses but now he well understood the Coyote's secretiveness. Their problems were only just beginning, and he'd be damned if he knew a way to solve any of them.

As the other man had stated, there wasn't a place on earth where they could truly find safety.

"Aiden." Del-Rey stopped him as he moved to enter the opening in the floor. Aiden turned back watching the other man carefully.

"If they conceive, the danger only worsens. What then?"

Aiden's eyes narrowed. "We don't wait, Rey. We show them now just how savage we can be in defending what is ours. We don't make mistakes and we keep the Code. Then we start praying. Because I have a feeling it's the only thing that's going to save us."

Chapter Thirty

ɛɔ

The scent of her need tempted him, pulled at him, filled his senses with the ambrosia of her heat. Aiden stepped into the small cave Del-Rey had made available for him and Charity. She waited on him, stretched out atop the mattress, watching him with hungry eyes as he closed the rough wooden door behind him.

Candlelight flickered over her features, highlighting the dark depths of her eyes, the creamy complexion of her skin. He could smell the light scent of soap and rainwater, proof that she had managed to browbeat the Coyote Breeds into arranging for a bath.

A sheet covered her from breast to thigh, leaving her long, tempting legs bare. His hands went to his shirt, stripping it off quickly as he reached the end of the bed. He could feel the blood beating hard and heavy through his body, his cock throbbing in demand.

The primitive need to complete the mating cycle, to take that final step, pounded in his brain, in his body. She was his mate. His woman. She had been taken from him, touched by another, no matter how impersonally, his hold on her severed for long, agonizing hours.

And more. To the bottom of his soul he believed Charity would conceive this night. Her scent was wilder, like spring nearing. A rebirth. Yet, he could tell her arousal was still heated, painful in her need.

Breed mating instinct had never been explained to him. Hell, no one had known it existed until just recently. Feeling his way through each phase of it was the hardest journey Aiden had ever taken. Facing what he prayed was this final phase, was the hardest. He needed her, his body clamored, demanding the final submission, and he was terrified she would refuse. Would he have the strength to walk away from her if she did?

He could feel his own lusts spiraling. Feel his needs burning through his body.

"Why are you waiting?" She tilted her head, watching him curiously.

He moved to the side of the bed, sitting down on the mattress slowly as he turned to face her. He would have preferred to wait till another time, but he knew his body, his instincts had finally marked the end of his patience.

He reached out to her, his fingers smoothing over her cheek, his thumb running over her lips.

"I need you," he whispered, grabbing desperately for his control to ease her into the coming experience.

"I don't understand." Her lips trembled nervously, her gaze flickering for just a moment, indicating that perhaps she did understand, or at least suspected.

He sighed roughly. "The mating is not complete, Charity. I've tried to wait, to give you time to accept the bonds between us, but I can wait no longer."

She drew in a hard, steady breath. "This is about the anal thing, isn't it?" She narrowed her eyes on him as her hands tightened on the sheet that covered her.

He grimaced, feeling her body tighten in rejection. "I will not do this without warning you first, Charity. I swear to you, I will not hurt you. I can do no more than that."

She arched a brow with insulting sarcasm. "You actually think it's going to fit?" she drawled mockingly.

Aiden couldn't help but smile. "I know it will, Charity. And soon, you'll know it as well."

The most endearing little pout sculpted her lips then. Aiden had not seen this particular expression on her face before. Equal parts determination and curiosity mixed with her disappointment that the loving she had expected would not be coming. She was burning for his touch, her body throbbing in need of release. The heat was an inferno in her cunt, her scent as wild and sweet as a summer thunderstorm.

"Aiden, did I neglect to tell you I'm really not into pain?" she finally asked him carefully, her tone filled with exaggerated patience. "I'm sure you couldn't have guessed it by now, but it doesn't rate very high on my list of things to experience."

He hid his smile. Her smart mouth was one of the things he most enjoyed about her.

"There will be no pain, Charity. I promise you, the moment you ask me to stop, I will do so willingly. But I bet," he whispered, "Once I start, you will be begging to continue rather than ease up in my possession of you."

"You'll stop if I need you to?" Her breathing had increased, her breasts rising and falling against the covering, her nipples poking against the cloth.

"If you need me to," he promised feeling his own breathing roughen, his cock so hard, so engorged with lust that the pain of it was nearly overwhelming. He could only pray he could maintain the control he needed not to harm her. "Just relax for me, Charity." He drew the sheet slowly from her body, staring into her eyes, keeping his voice soft, low, comforting. "Just relax and feel."

She swallowed tightly. "Yeah well, the feeling part is what's starting to worry me," she gasped as he lowered his head, lips covering the mark on her shoulder. "Oh hell. I guess we'll find out now if it really is an exit only."

Aiden chuckled. He couldn't help himself. He could hear her nervousness, her arousal and her acceptance of what was coming in the tone of her voice. Her hands gripped his forearms as he stroked his tongue over the mark he had left on her, relishing the sweet, slightly tangy taste of her skin.

Her body was soft and delicate in his arms and he couldn't help the unfamiliar surge of emotions that welled within him. He held on to her, his hands moving to her back as he drew her closer in his arms, needing to hold her, to know she was safe, secure.

He remembered clearly that blinding fury that had surged through his soul when he realized she had been taken. Fear. He had never known fear in his life until that moment. The thought of his own death did little to affect him. The thought of so much as the slightest added pain to the delicate body in his arms sent his primal senses thundering with the need for violence. The need to mark in that final, ultimate surrender.

"I lost my mind when I realized you were gone," he whispered at her ear, feeling her tremble in surprise. "I have never howled in my life, Charity. But the moment I realized you were missing, even the wolves knew my rage."

They had answered the primal call. They had tracked the jeep as it made its way up the mountain, then returned the news of its location as it stopped. Primal instinct, sharp, flashing, a communication with the animals he had never expected.

"I was frightened," she whispered. "I prayed you would find me, Aiden."

"And I did," he growled. He couldn't stop the vibration that echoed through his voice. "I have to finish this now, Charity. I have to complete the mating. Now."

He couldn't explain it. It made no sense. The act of anal sex would not aid in conception. The hormone in his semen would in no way affect anything to further mark her. Yet, he couldn't deny the impulse. He wanted to turn her instantly to her stomach, raise her hips and mount her immediately. Assure himself that she was his, completely his, submitting to the sexuality between them, accepting the mating they shared.

And he feared it was from there that the overwhelming need was bred. The need, the overwhelming compulsion to assure himself that his mate was his alone. That she would submit to his every need. That she would give herself, no matter how he needed her.

His lips covered hers as he fought the baser instinct to take her quickly. His tongue probed her mouth, stroking over hers, licking at her teeth, her lips, growling fiercely until she drew on him, suckling at the swollen glands at the side of his tongue.

He moaned as he felt the release of the hormone, his cock jerking at the thought that within minutes her needs would outstretch his, her arousal becoming an inferno that would burn them both in the cataclysm.

"Aiden, wait." She pulled back from him, breathing heavy, fighting for control. He knew she was fighting for control. Fighting to analyze the responses of her body, to understand the actions and reactions of their sexuality.

He didn't want the scientist in his bed that night. He wanted the woman. His mate. Her fiery heat searing him, her juices flowing with her need. He growled at her, his lips lifting in a snarl as his fingers tangled in her hair, holding her still as his lips took her again.

When she refused to suckle his tongue into her mouth, he nipped at her lips until they parted with a hot gasp. He could feel her body growing hotter, smell the rich, feminine scent of her arousal wrapping around him, drowning him in the scent of her lusts.

His head tilted, his lips slanting over hers as he finally allowed her to release him. She was panting for breath, her hands kneading his shoulders as she rubbed her hard tipped breasts against his naked chest, as one hand slid down his abdomen to grip the shaft of his cock.

He grimaced, throwing his head back as her finger stroked the heavy veins and pulsing flesh. The agony of his desire was like nothing he had known before. It tightened his body, coursed through his veins and tingled up his spine with a pleasure that surpassed anything he had heard rumor of.

"Enough." He gripped her fingers, pulling them back from his needy flesh as he pushed her to the bed. "This is for you, Charity. All for you. You may give to me later."

"No." She stared up at him, her eyes dazed, almost black with her desire. "I need to touch you, Aiden."

"Not yet, love," he soothed her gently as he moved beside her, his palm cupping a swollen breast with the utmost gentleness. "Relax, Charity. Just feel, baby. For me. Just feel all the sensations I can bring to your body."

Then he could resist no longer. His head lowered, his mouth covering the elongated nipple awaiting his attention. He felt her body jerk, heard the tumultuous cry that escaped her lips and knew that before the night was over, she would never deny the mating again.

Chapter Thirty-One

છ

Charity hadn't realized how frightened she had been until Aiden had arrived within the caverns. His strong arms had wrapped around her, his muscular body sheltering her, holding her in a way that reassured her, protected her. She hadn't realized how much she needed his strength until he had entered, expecting her, needing her to lean on him.

And now he needed so much more. She trembled as she watched his head lower to the breast he cupped in his hand. She couldn't restrain the near violent jerk of her body, or the gasping indrawn breath when the heat of his mouth enclosed the hard tip.

His tongue curled around her nipple, drawing a desperate moan from her throat as her hands gripped at his shoulders. She could do nothing but feel, as he wanted her to. Nothing but ride the wave of sexuality and pleasure he was inflicting on her heated senses.

His long, knowing fingers kneaded her sensitive breasts as his tongue licked the hard, pointed tip in time to the deep suckling motions of his mouth. Then he moved over her further, his hands pressing the full mounds of her breasts together, drawing the two hard nipples together as his mouth covered both.

"Aiden, damn you. You're killing me." She was fighting for breath, for her sanity, but her hands were locked in his hair, holding him close to her as her body arched closer to the heated caress.

Her head tossed on the mattress as sensation swelled inside her. Like a lava-hot tidal wave, it began to build within her womb, stronger, more intense than ever before.

She could feel her juices sliding from her cunt, dampening the bare folds like hot honey. Her clit throbbed, pleaded for attention. Her vagina clenched spasmodically, demanding the hard throbbing length of his cock. She whimpered with that need as he gave her nipples a final lick before his lips began to travel lower.

Her fingers clenched in his hair as his canines raked the perspiration-damp skin of her abdomen. Then her breath caught in her throat as he blew a breath of heated air across her pulsing clit.

"Please," she whispered, lifting her hips to him, needing his tongue on the small nerve center as desperately as she needed air to breathe.

"I want to taste you first," he whispered as he moved between her thighs slowly, his eyes dark, cloudy with desire as he spread her legs, encouraging her to bend her knees and open herself to him.

She watched him, helpless in the grip of the sensations swelling through her body. She watched as his long graceful fingers caressed her thighs, then his head lowered. His tongue distended then swiped slowly through the narrow, soaked slit of her pussy.

She shuddered. Her body quaked with the intensity of pleasure that engulfed her senses. Her head fell back to the bed, her eyes closing as her hips lifted to him.

"More," she begged, panting, nearly mindless in the grip of sensations washing over her. Heat flickered at her cunt, traveled through her womb, wrapped around her breasts. Like unseen, taunting fingers it stroked over her body, fanning the flames higher.

His hands smoothed over her thighs and the muscles there trembled as he drew slowly closer to the damp folds of flesh he was feasting ravenously at. His tongue flickered through the sensitized slit teasingly, circled her swollen clit then flickered down again to rim the clenching entrance to her vagina. Like a slow, careful figure eight, a teasing, seductive dance of fire, he stroked and licked, drawing the silky juices from her cunt, holding her open, allowing them to slide heatedly to the entrance of her anus.

She knew what was coming. Her brain sounded a warning that was lost amid the suckling, licking caresses of his lips and tongue. And she thought it could get no worse. Thought she had reached the pinnacle of need, until he showed her otherwise.

She felt his hand move as his tongue tempted her clit. One long, graceful finger slid into the tight entrance of her greedy pussy. She tried to clench her thighs, to trap his finger inside her, but his broad shoulders held her open as his warning growl had her shuddering in heated response.

Her hips lifted as she fought to draw him deeper inside. She needed him moving, plunging his finger inside her to free the taut need spiraling within her womb. Yet he only teased, drawing her higher, stoking the fires to a desperate pitch as her cries echoed around them.

She was so desperate, poised so close to the edge of orgasm that she opened naturally for the finger that slid to her anus and pressed slowly inside.

"Aiden," she chanted his name as she felt the digit fill her, slowly stretching her, preparing her. Even more frightening was the sudden, intense pleasure that washed over her, as he stroked in and out, accustoming her to the feel of being invaded.

"You are so pretty, Charity," he growled. "So flushed and responsive, you make me nearly lose control, when I need to hold onto it."

She felt a second finger join the first. Working inside her tight depths, as the muscles clenched on his fingers. The streaking wash of pleasure/pain had her fighting for the nearing climax she could feel burning in her womb. She twisted in his grip, her hands falling from his head to the blankets beneath her as she fought to hold onto reality.

She was pressing against each stroke into her anus now, gasping, feeling the vibrations of the entrance tease at her hungry cunt. If only he would fill her, fuck her to orgasm before he decided to try to destroy her sanity.

"I can't stand this." She wanted to scream but she had barely the breath to whimper pleadingly. "Please, Aiden. Don't tease me like this any longer."

"I could sip from your honey for hours," he whispered, licking into the clenching entrance of her cunt as she shivered beneath him.

Then his tongue plunged inside her, separating sensitized muscles and sending tremors of her nearing orgasm washing over her. When his tongue drew back he rose from between her thighs, his fingers sliding from the hot depths of her anus.

"Turn over for me," he bit out. "I won't last much longer, Charity. Submit to me now."

Her eyes widened. The words, the tone of voice, were more primal than ever before. His features were etched with savage lust, his eyes glittering with a hunger, a need that couldn't be missed. This had nothing to do with a sexual fetish and everything to do with sexual submission. His desires were now instinctive. He was her mate and he was getting ready to prove it to her.

She turned slowly. Her heart was racing in her chest; lust pounding in her veins, burning her with her own needs. And there was Aiden, his hands turning her as he moved quickly behind her.

There were few preliminaries. The need was like fire searing their nerve endings, drowning them in the drive for release. Hard hands smoothed over the curves of her rear as she shuddered before him. One moved up her back, caressing up her spine before applying pressure between her shoulders to indicate he wanted them lowered. She was left with her upper body cushioned on the mattress, her rear raised, unprotected before his heated gaze.

Chapter Thirty-Two

೮೧

Candlelight flickered over the room as lust steamed around them. Charity knew she should have been nervous, should have been shaking with fear. She knew what he was about to do couldn't actually be done. The thick length of his cock was too large, her anus too small. Her fingers clenched in the sheet beneath her. She couldn't deny the erotic, sexual tension that invaded her at the thought, though.

"So pretty," his words whispered over her as she felt her cunt burn in response to the fingers that moved over the curves of her buttocks, his thumbs sliding down the cleft between them.

Charity could feel her body burning. Shudders of arousal shook her muscles, weakening her as Aiden moved into position behind her.

"Slow and easy, baby," he whispered as she felt the head of his cock nudge against the entrance to her anus.

She would have preferred that her body appear less desperate for the primal impalement, but she could feel her muscles relaxing, her greedy body attempting to open for him.

Charity whimpered in desperation as she felt the head of his cock flex and throb then she jerked in surprise as she felt the heated pulse of fluid that shot into the entrance of her anus.

"Easy." His voice was guttural. One hand clamped to the side of her buttock; holding her still, he paused with just the tip of his cock buried at the entrance.

Amazingly, shockingly, Charity felt the slick fluid heating the entrance, lubricating it as it slowly relaxed her muscles. She knew she should fight to hold onto enough sanity to figure out what the hell was happening to her body, but the arousal growing inside her had a mind of its own.

She pressed against the velvety crown of his cock as she felt her entrance relax further, crying out as the head buried inside her, stretching her, burning the tender, untried muscles there as they stretched to accommodate the width of his cock.

He paused. She could hear him breathing, the sound rough and hot in her ears as she realized he was fighting for his own control. Another pulse of the fluid filled her then, the silky fire blazing into her anus, igniting nerve endings, sensitizing them even as it relaxed her muscles further. She felt him slide deeper into the dark channel as a fiery wash of pleasure/pain attacked her sensitized body.

The hard, heated pulses of fluid seemed to relax each muscle, allowing her body to accommodate the size of the invader stretching it so deliciously. She clenched her muscles around Aiden's cock, hearing him groan with a rush of pleasure as she caressed in turn.

His hands gripped her hips, his fingers kneading the flesh as she felt him slide deeper, deeper, until with a final thrust he was buried to the hilt inside the hot depths of her ass.

Charity was shaking as she felt him cover her. His upper body lowered over her back, his teeth scraping the mark at her shoulder as his tongue swiped over it soothingly.

"God, you're hot, Charity," he growled at her ear. "So hot my cock is on fire from it."

His hips flexed, drawing his cock back several inches before thrusting forward once again. Charity cried out at the deep, forbidden caress as she felt the flames in her body burning higher, hotter. She couldn't think, couldn't make sense of the depth of arousal churning in her womb.

"Yeah, tighten on me, baby," he gasped as she did just that. "Ah hell. Charity. You're killing me."

The words sent a fist punch of reaction into her womb, shocking her with the power of the pleasure she was receiving from his cock buried up her ass.

She was filled with him. Her flesh stretched so tightly around him that she could feel the throb of each pulse of his cock into her cunt. The fluid that still shot in her ass had her slick, lubricated so well that there was no stress to her muscles as he began to move inside her.

"Aiden." She flexed her muscles around his erection. It hurt, yet it was the most incredible pleasure she had ever known.

"There, baby," he growled, thrusting back into her, his thick cock taking her anal channel easily. "We'll do this nice and easy, baby."

At first, slow and gentle, leaving them both gasping with the need for more. But within minutes her cries were filling the room as his thrusts began to increase. His cock stroked inside her, back and forth, alternately soothing and inflaming the nerve endings there as he fucked her with slow easy strokes. But the needs growing inside her refused to be quenched by such an easy possession.

She tightened the muscles of her anus, clenching and stroking his cock as his breathing roughened further. He was nearly gasping for breath now, joining her in the insanity of arousal beginning to overtake them.

"Stop," he growled. "For God's sake, Charity. You keep milking my cock like that and I won't be responsible..." His groan was harsh, broken as she tightened again, her hips undulating beneath him as she fought for more of the heated strokes of pleasure/pain that each thrust brought.

"More," she moaned, pressing back into the possession. "Harder, Aiden. Oh God, fuck me harder." She couldn't believe it. There was no way she could live through such intensity, such a level of pleasure and pain combined.

His cock surged into her ass, parting the muscles with a stroke of pinching pain, then sinking into the hot depth with a lightning stroke of agonizing pleasure.

He began to move faster. He drew his cock back slowly from the tight grip she had on it, their cries mingling in the steamy air around them. But when he pushed forward again, Charity fought to keep from screaming with the intensity of sensations. The hard, forceful strokes awoke such an intense driving need for more that she became helpless in its grip.

She knew later she would blush from the memory of how desperately she began to beg. Even as he began to move inside her, his thrusts increasing in speed, in desperation, she begged.

Charity couldn't still the hunger raging through her. The intense pleasure, the pure eroticism of the act was too much for her to comprehend, to make sense of. All she knew was that each driving stroke, each hard thrust was throwing her closer, driving her higher to a pinnacle of pleasure she was desperate to reach.

Her back bowed, her hips tilted back, her muscles clenched on the impaling cock as yet more of the slick fluid shot into her greedy ass. His cock surged inside her, fucking her with a deep, driving rhythm. She trembled, shaking, screaming out at the sensations as he pushed one hand beneath her body, his fingers moving to her swollen clit as he began to pound into her harder, faster, torturing her anal channel with each stroke. She was on fire, the pleasure building until a painful inferno of need burned through her body.

She could feel his stroking fingers driving her clit closer to explosion. The hard thrusts up her ass driving her to mindless, insane lust. Each pulse of the heated fluid from the tip of his cock made her hungry for more. Made her desperate for the hot, surging explosion of his sperm inside her instead.

"Now, Charity. Now, baby." His fingers stroked the bundle of nerves carefully, just the right pressure, two quick strokes and she exploded.

She felt her ass clench, tighten on his flesh a second before she heard his heated cry, felt his teeth lock into her shoulder. And she would have been terrified. Should have been screaming in fear as she felt the thick swelling of the knot surge inside her already overfilled ass.

She would have… Instead, she screamed out at the blinding pleasure as the engorged knot seemed to fill her pussy, tightening her muscles there, sending a surge of cascading sensations clear to her womb. The orgasm that shook through her destroyed her. It was never ending, a quaking inferno of lust, of pleasure/pain, of fiery satisfaction unlike anything she could have imagined.

She felt the eruption of his sperm into her anus. A hard, almost brutal jerk of his body that tugged at the anchoring knot as his seed poured into her. Another climax rippled over her before the first could ease away, throwing her back into the abyss of sensation once again.

It would never end. She was crying weakly, helpless in the grip of her body's driving response to this primal possession. How her fragile anus accommodated his size as well as the hard swelling she didn't know, she didn't care. It was taking every inch with greedy pleasure as her cunt erupted time and again from each explosion of seed from his cock, each hard throb of the knot that echoed into her sensitized pussy.

She collapsed weakly beneath him, shudders of her echoing orgasm still tearing through her as she felt the swelling slowly recede. He drew back from her then, his cock dragging through the sensitive tissue as she whimpered weakly from the nearly painful pleasure it caused.

She lay dazed, weak as he moved from the bed to the pitcher of water that sat in a metal basin across the room. She heard water cascade into the large bowl, the sounds of it splashing, then silence. Seconds later his hands touched her and she groaned as he drew the cool cloth between her thighs, cleaning her gently.

Aiden was tender, as gentle as he knew how to be as he cleaned her. His large hands weren't demanding or in any way trying to evoke a response. But one came anyway. Within minutes she was moving beneath his hand, her drowsy moans marking her need. She was tired, worn, but her immediate response triggered his own.

There were no preliminaries as he moved between her thighs. His cock was hard, his breathing as heavy as hers, and the drive to take her again was quickly making him insane.

He pushed into her soaked pussy. Hearing her gasp, moan as she tightened around him. He knew her weariness was a deep as her need, and he moved quickly to ease one so the other could overtake her.

"God, you're so fucking tight, Charity," he whispered, his hands gripping her hips as he stared at where his body possessed her. "So hot and wet I could drown in you."

"Drown," she moaned weakly. "Fuck me, Aiden. Now. Hard." She was whimpering with her need, with her arousal as her cunt clenched around his erection.

He leaned into her, holding her against his body as he began to pump inside her. His eyes closed as the fist tight heat clamped on his cock. Slick fire, the pulse of the lubricating fluid from his cock making her hotter, wetter, but the tightened muscles never let go of his flesh.

He was gasping for breath as he thrust inside her. His erection was brutally hard, sensitized, and only seconds from exploding when he felt the quaking shudders rush through her body and her own climax overtaking her.

He followed her swiftly, barely containing his cry of pleasure as he felt his cock swell, filling her, arching her body as he locked inside her, his seed spewing into the rich depths of her body as she slowly stilled beneath him.

His hands soothed her, eased her into sleep even before he was able to pull his cock from her tight grip and collapse beside her. Satisfaction unlike anything he had known washed over him then. It settled through his body, warmed his soul. And as he looked down at her, he knew he loved her. Knew he had loved her even years before, when he thought he had hated her.

He kissed her cheek as he pulled her closer to his body and allowed himself to drift slowly into rest. As long as she was safe, he could sleep.

Chapter Thirty-Three

ຽວ

Her scent had definitely changed. Aiden lay, hours later after coming awake, staring up at the ceiling as his senses picked up the slow change within her body. She lay with her back against his chest, his arms wrapped around her as he kept her warm, comforted, and noted the conception taking place.

Rather than a scent that reminded him of a storm breaking across the mountains, this one reminded him of spring, of warm, surging life. His eyes closed as his hand moved to her flat abdomen, his fingers spreading across the warm expanse of flesh.

His eyes closed as he allowed the truth to wash over him. He had loved her before, fiercely, heatedly, but what he felt now overwhelmed emotions only barely being recognized. He stared across the room at the rough table, the rock wall, a frown creasing his brow as he wondered at the often confusing impulses that ran rife through his system.

He had rarely known tenderness. Had no use for softness. Yet he found he could treat Charity no other way. Everything in him softened for her, and that terrified him. Terrified and exhilarated him.

He stared down at her face, sighing softly at the clench of his heart. How many times had he scoffed at Wolfe and Jacob for their attitudes toward their mates? Hell, he had flat-out laughed at Wolfe for giving into Hope's desire for a wedding. And yet, here he lay, knowing if Charity asked for such a thing, no matter how much the social practices of those who reviled him, irked at him, he would do it.

She had conceived. He could feel the knowledge to the soles of his feet. In the last hours as he held her, the change had taken place within her body. What had triggered it, if anything had, he wasn't certain. But as he thought about it, considered the overriding need to take her in the most elemental manner, he thought that perhaps instinctively, he had known. He had known that the process was slowly evolving, her body accepting his seed, and he had needed to mark her in that final way, to impress upon her how tightly they were bound.

It made sense now. Wolfe and Jacob hadn't yet seen what Aiden now saw. The need to take their mates anally had nothing to do with the changes their bodies were making. It was due to the fact that during ovulation, their senses were so well-honed, so aware that their mates were evolving to perfect fertility that they went into overload. The need for sexual submission forged a desire that would otherwise not be so imperative. It was primal. Animalistic. And it offered no apologies.

Sighing deeply, he dragged himself away from her, tucking the thick quilt around her body and pulling himself to his feet. Dawn was only hours away, and there was much to do.

The information he learned here changed several plans he, Wolfe and Jacob had been trying to find time to implement. It also raised the question of the Breed Code and how far they were willing to go to enforce it. The woman who had betrayed them had signed her agreement to it and apparently, willingly betrayed them. The thought of killing a woman, especially one so young, was abhorrent to him.

He dressed slowly, the reality of the Breeds' lives a heavy burden on his soul. How would they ever fit into the world when their very DNA marked them as different, animalistic? They weren't seen as completely human, even by those who aided them. He smelled their fear, their distrust. Such basic human responses always resulted in bloodshed, eventually.

He gazed down at Charity one last time, every muscle in his body protesting the need to leave her for even a short time. Then he shook his head, still a little confused at how easily she had wormed her way into his soul, as he strode quickly from the small cave.

The interconnecting tunnels and caves were the product of a gold mining venture from nearly a century past. Every drop of ore had been mined from the once rich veins that had run through the mountain, leaving in its place a system of caves and tunnels that the Coyotes had slowly marked as a home.

The main tunnel was wider than the others and led back to the main cavern where Wolf and Coyote Breeds mingled in reluctant camaraderie. Their fight was now the same, but there were still questions to be answered.

The Coyote Breeds that inhabited the caves lacked the rancid smell of the Council mongrels that obeyed the whims of their creators. Aiden had often suspected that the evil of those men were what produced the smell of death that lay about them like an aura of shame. Del-Rey's Coyotes, like all Breeds, had their own distinctive scent, wild, untamed, but without the scent of carnage.

It was perplexing, the laws of nature that were beginning to apply within the different Breeds and the framework of the almost instinctive code of honor they held. Coyotes in nature, knew little honor, unlike the Wolf, and Felines that most Breeds were related to. Coyotes were known to have no soul. Yet in this instance, with the Coyote Breeds of this pack, it seemed the human spirit itself had made up for the lack.

"Aiden, Wolfe has the situation back at the compound under control. The woman is being watched and all relays from her station are being monitored. She slipped out a report several hours ago of Charity's death," Hawke reported, his voice dark and filled with menace.

Aiden sighed in resignation. "Get ready to move out in one hour." He turned to Del-Rey.

Del-Rey was leaning against the wall, his arms crossed over his chest, watching Aiden through dark, emotionless eyes.

"You are welcome to return to the compound," he told him. "The problem of the woman you've kidnapped could cause you problems, though. You may be forced to return her."

Del-Rey smiled, though it was more a snarl. "I don't think that will be happening, Aiden. I know now what I needed to know. We will stay here. Perhaps our Packs could work together, though. I believe such a union would benefit us all."

Aiden nodded shortly. "We'll see about getting you some equipment up here. I have several ideas I'll discuss with Wolfe first. We need to move carefully, Del-Rey. World opinion could turn against the Breeds as easily as it has worked for us."

The other man tilted his head in acknowledgement. Aiden had a feeling working with him could be more difficult than working with the government liaisons who drove the Breeds crazy.

"I'll contact you soon then. Get a list together of supplies you need, equipment, whatever. Let's see about helping each other instead of working against each other. Assign one of your men to the compound; I'll leave one of mine here to coordinate as well. I have a feeling time is of the essence now."

Del-Rey nodded as he straightened from his slouch position and moved to several of his men to begin getting things together.

"Hawke, contact Wolfe," Aiden told him quietly. "I want that woman secured before I head in with Charity. We'll deal with her on our return."

Hawke's eyes flashed, his expression hardening as though he would protest the order before he nodded abruptly and turned away. Whatever was on the other man's mind would have to wait.

"Nikki." The doctor sat at the table watching the meeting with curious, dark eyes.

She rose to her feet and walked to him slowly. She watched his expression carefully, he noted, her own somber and intense.

"Charity?" His throat closed up. Son of a bitch, this overload of emotion was more than aggravation.

"She's conceived," she said a bit too loudly. "I figured it would happen soon."

He watched her questioningly as her lips quirked somberly. "Too many changes in her body too quickly." She shrugged. "Let's hope conception eases her inability to be touched. We'll have to watch this closely, Aiden." He could see her fears, her worries. He nodded shortly, clenching his jaw against his own fears. "We'll be leaving here soon. Find out what they need in the way of medical supplies so we can get those together. We may have more need of them than we could imagine right now. We have to keep her safe." And there lay his greatest fear.

"Yes we do," she sighed tiredly. "Her safety, Aiden, must become the Pack's ultimate goal. I'll be done quickly. I had already anticipated your order. I've found at times, you Breeds can be highly predictable."

"And I've found they can be highly irritating." Aiden turned in surprise at the sound of Charity's voice.

She stood in the entrance to the room, dressed and ready to fight. Her face was flushed, her eyes glittering with anger.

"When were you going to tell me?" she asked him with a tone of forced patience as the rest of the occupants turned to watch the confrontation.

He grinned. He could see the telltale emotion in her gaze, the love she thought she kept so carefully hidden from him. He shrugged negligently.

"When were *you* going to tell *me*?" He tried to keep his voice stern. "Do you think I'm unaware of the fact that you suspected this before the attack that you were ovulating? Come, Charity, I may be male, but I'm hardly stupid."

Her face flushed. "I wasn't certain."

"Of course you were," Nikki jumped into the fray. "Otherwise you wouldn't have been so reticent over the exam I wanted to perform. Really, Charity, all you had to do was say something." Her voice was smoothly mocking.

Charity frowned at her friend fiercely as she crossed her arms over her chest.

"Perhaps I was waiting for more than a damned mating," she bit out furiously, though he could hear the hurt behind her words as she speared him with another look. "I didn't say I accepted that submission stuff either, Aiden," she bit out. "You say I'm your mate. I don't."

He chuckled then. He paid little attention to the men who watched him or their interest in the confrontation as he moved quickly to her. He caught her around her waist, pulling her flush against his body, allowing her to feel the erection that had not yet truly eased.

"I say you are my heart," he said clearly. "And if you remember correctly, I told you this before either of us suspected the change, Charity."

She frowned. "Someone has to be, because it's clear you don't have one," she sniped trying to pull away from him.

He shook his head, more than a little confused as he stared down at her.

"I love you, Charity, what more do you want?" He frowned as she suddenly stilled in his arms.

"You what?" she whispered faintly. "Say it again."

He smiled down at her, amused, so filled with his love for her that at times he wondered how he could hold it all.

"I love you, mate," he growled as he lowered his head until his nose touched hers. "See what is as plain as the nose on your face. You are my heart, Charity. My soul. My mate."

As slow as the dawn, as gentle as a summer morning her smile washed across her face, though she tried to narrow her eyes in intimidation, nothing could still the joy he saw spreading through her.

"Fine. I guess I'll let you be my mate then." She went to push away from him.

"I don't think so." He pulled her back. "I expect a bit more than that after making me declare myself in front of Coyotes." He was more than aware of snickers sounding behind him.

She peeked over his shoulder, a smile tugging at her lips as she returned her gaze to him.

"Yeah, they are kind of amused," she said softly. "But their day will come."

"That wasn't what I'm waiting for." His hand slid to her rear as he patted it warningly. "Surely you have more to say?"

"Well," she drawled. "I would tell you how much I love you, but right now that hand patting my ass is a little too arrogant. Rein it in."

His brow arched. She filled him with joy, but he could tell it would be no small matter to keep the upper hand with her. His hand tightened on the tempting curve of her buttock as he lifted her closer. She gasped as his thigh pressed against the soft mound of her pussy. He could feel her heat, and then he could smell it. Natural, needy, a heady scent that went to his head faster than any drug.

"I love you," she breathed out, suddenly serious, her eyes moist with emotion, velvet soft with feeling. "I always have, Aiden."

His arms tightened her around her, his head lowering to catch her lips in a kiss that seared his soul. It was no more than his lips to her lips as his eyes stared into hers. No more than the meeting of souls.

In that moment Aiden knew that the gift of her love, given so long before, was all that had driven him.

Unknowingly, instinctively, he had known that only she could light the bleak dark corners of who and what he was. And she filled it, lighting it with such emotion and such need, it nearly drove him to his knees.

"We have an audience," she whispered against his lips.

"Fuck 'em," he grunted as his hands smoothed up her back, his heart glorying in her, in the many gifts she had given him.

"No." She laughed then, joy spreading through her face. "Fuck me instead. Later. Maybe on a beanbag again?"

"You liked the beanbag," he murmured as his body tightened at the thought. Keeping his arm around her, he turned quickly to face the snickering group watching him. "Well, Rey, it's been informative. But it's time for us to go. Get your lists together, visit when you can." He drew Charity to the tunnel as she laughed behind him. "Hawke, assign someone here and get your ass to the jeep or I'm leaving without you."

It was time to go home. But damned if he knew where he was going to find another beanbag on such short notice. Maybe he could improvise, he thought. Surely there was something similar.

Epilogue

❧

They had locked her into a room by herself. A steel enclosed room. No doors. No windows. There was no view out, but the large two-way mirror provided a view in. What Hawke saw bit at his soul.

The woman was slender, compact, staring silently from the fold-down cot she lay on. Her big blue eyes glittered with moisture but no tears had fallen in the hours she had been confined there. Resignation and acceptance lay over her like a cloak of pain.

He had come to the small, dark room to watch her as soon as he returned to the compound. He needed to see her to reaffirm to himself that the decision he was faced with could be carried out.

The Army hadn't been notified of her betrayal. That was Faith's job and after one long searching look when he had asked her to delay the message, she had nodded her agreement. Now he stood here, merely watching, unable to step past the door at the end of the long room and give her the go ahead to do so.

Was it a difference in how he was trained, he wondered? He hadn't experienced the unjust cruelties that many of the other Breeds had faced. He had been created, observed, tested and trained by professionals. By men and women who understood that the true answers came from caring treatment. It hadn't been enough for him. The assignments he had been sent on were bloody, vicious, and he had been expected to perform with a lack of mercy.

He had done as he was ordered but always with an eye on the best opportunity to escape. When the time came he had gladly taken it. But he didn't hold the bitter, painful memories of abuse such as Wolfe, Jacob and the other Breeds held. He understood it. He accepted it. He knew their lives hung in the balance of world opinion at the moment, and that tide could change any day. He was willing to give his life for those who had adopted him. He was willing to fight for their greater freedom. But he wasn't willing to kill his mate.

Fuck! When had he accepted her as his mate, he wondered. When had he finally given in to the subtle demand his body was making on his mind?

She brushed at her cheek, wiping away a tear that had finally fallen. Her people didn't know they had locked her away. When he called in the order he had been precise. Confine her secretly. Let no one know she had been taken or where she was being held.

He watched the door to her room open. She stood to attention slowly, warily, blinking as Wolfe and his mate, Hope, walked into the room. They were a powerful pair. Hope's tall, striking good looks with their slightly Asian cast made her appear cool, untouchable as she preceded Wolfe into the room.

Wolfe was over six inches taller, heavily muscled, a powerful dangerous force to be reckoned with. His dark skin and long black hair appeared Native American. His blue eyes and cruel slash of a mouth made him look primordially dangerous.

"Jessica." Wolfe nodded to her as he and Hope walked to the table that sat several feet from the cot and sat down. "Sit down, please."

Wolfe pushed the extra chair from beneath the table with his foot as he watched her. Hawke saw the fear that flashed in her eyes. She paled for a moment, her lower lip trembling as she walked over and took her seat.

She stared forward, not defiantly, but rather somberly. She had accepted her fate.

"Jessica, would you like to tell us why you betrayed us?" Hope's voice was gentle, soft.

Hawke watched Jessica flinch from the caring tone. She glanced at Wolfe then. He was watching her intently, his expression cold, forbidding.

"I have no excuse." Her voice was husky, rough from unshed tears. It caused pain to lash through his gut, taking his breath with the need to rush into the room to protect her, if nothing else, from her fears.

Hawke was aware of Jacob walking up and standing beside him then. Moving silently to the glass, watching the proceedings broodingly.

"You sent a message that Charity had died. That you yourself had seen the body. You pulled Hope and Faith into the communications building with you using a very weak excuse." Wolfe's tone had her flinching with his anger. "I do not believe you wanted to see our women harmed, Jessica. Yet still, you gave your father the coordinates to our personal homes and allowed that attack. Why?" He bared his teeth, the sharp canines at the side of his mouth drawing her gaze.

Hawke watched her pale further as she swallowed with a sick tightness. Her creamy skin was snow white now, her dark blue eyes nearly black with fear. Her gaze flickered to Hope.

"I did all I could," she whispered faintly. "To minimize damage."

Wolfe leaned forward slowly, dangerously. A smooth ripple of motion that had her jerking, a whimper of fear breaking from her throat.

"You signed the Code," he said harshly as she trembled before him. "You knew the consequences."

Hawke's hands tightened to fists as the need to protect her surged through his body.

"I knew the consequences." For all its faintness, her voice was strong. "I accept them."

"Death," Wolfe bit out ferociously. "Death, Jessica. An execution. Were you prepared for that?"

Her eyes closed briefly before she turned her head, staring at the leader of the Packs, regret and unbearable pain shining in her eyes.

"I was prepared for that, Pack Leader," she whispered. "I knew the consequences are death."

In that moment, Hawke felt his soul shatter.

Why an electronic book?

We live in the Information Age—an exciting time in the history of human civilization, in which technology rules supreme and continues to progress in leaps and bounds every minute of every day. For a multitude of reasons, more and more avid literary fans are opting to purchase e-books instead of paper books. The question from those not yet initiated into the world of electronic reading is simply: *Why?*

1. *Price.* An electronic title at Ellora's Cave Publishing and Cerridwen Press runs anywhere from 40% to 75% less than the cover price of the exact same title in paperback format. Why? Basic mathematics and cost. It is less expensive to publish an e-book (no paper and printing, no warehousing and shipping) than it is to publish a paperback, so the savings are passed along to the consumer.

2. *Space.* Running out of room in your house for your books? That is one worry you will never have with electronic books. For a low one-time cost, you can purchase a handheld device specifically designed for e-reading. Many e-readers have large, convenient screens for viewing. Better yet, hundreds of titles can be stored within your new library—on a single microchip. There are a variety of e-readers from different manufacturers. You can also read e-books on your PC or laptop computer. (Please note that Ellora's Cave does not endorse any specific brands.

You can check our websites at www.ellorascave.com or www.cerridwenpress.com for information we make available to new consumers.)

3. *Mobility.* Because your new e-library consists of only a microchip within a small, easily transportable e-reader, your entire cache of books can be taken with you wherever you go.

4. *Personal Viewing Preferences.* Are the words you are currently reading too small? Too large? Too… ANNOYING? Paperback books cannot be modified according to personal preferences, but e-books can.

5. *Instant Gratification.* Is it the middle of the night and all the bookstores near you are closed? Are you tired of waiting days, sometimes weeks, for bookstores to ship the novels you bought? Ellora's Cave Publishing sells instantaneous downloads twenty-four hours a day, seven days a week, every day of the year. Our webstore is never closed. Our e-book delivery system is 100% automated, meaning your order is filled as soon as you pay for it.

Those are a few of the top reasons why electronic books are replacing paperbacks for many avid readers.

As always, Ellora's Cave and Cerridwen Press welcome your questions and comments. We invite you to email us at Comments@ellorascave.com or write to us directly at Ellora's Cave Publishing Inc., 1056 Home Avenue, Akron, OH 44310-3502.

COMING TO A BOOKSTORE NEAR YOU!

ELLORA'S CAVE

Bestselling Authors Tour

erridwen, the Celtic Goddess of wisdom, was the muse who brought inspiration to story-tellers and those in the creative arts. Cerridwen Press encompasses the best and most innovative stories in all genres of today's fiction. Visit our site and discover the newest titles by talented authors who still get inspired - much like the ancient storytellers did, once upon a time.

Cerridwen Press

www.cerridwenpress.com